A
Quint Cord
Novel

Bear Tracks

Betty J. Vaughn

TotalRecall Publications, Inc.
1103 Middlecreek
Friendswood, Texas 77546
281-992-3131 TEL
www.totalrecallpress.com

ISBN: 978-1-64883-258-1
UPC: 6-43977-42581-2

Library of Congress Control Number: 2023936179

FIRST EDITION
1   2   3   4   5   6   7   8   9   10

There are those that we meet in life that become an integral part of our history. Such a one is my Jr. and Sr. high school friend, college roommate, lifelong friend, and now editor. She is always bubbly, enthusiastic, and projects happiness regardless of worrisome issues she may be facing. Quite simply, I have always loved Dr. Judith Conway Gordon. I am indebted to her for her support of my books and her encouragement.

Author's Bio

Betty J. Vaughn has written all of her life, winning awards in school and afterwards. Following a career teaching AP art history and painting, she wrote her first novel, Yesterday's Magnolia, quickly followed by four historical novels. The Man in the Chimney; Turbulent Waters; Run, Cissy, Run, and The Intrepid Miss LaRoque. The four novels in the historical series were all winners of the award for historical fiction from the NC Society of Historians as was the biography, The Mystery of Sarah Slater. The latest Quint Cord novel, deals with concerns that currently plague our Nation as well as many others. A graduate of East Carolina University and a prize winning watercolorist, Mrs. Vaughn is a resident of Raleigh, NC, enjoys traveling, gardening, gourmet cooking, and reading. She is currently researching for her next book.

"Mrs. Vaughn can consider herself a seasoned novelist. Her books are fast paced, action packed, and full of adventure. Her work isn't just a flurry of words, dry and boring. She is a master of literary technique as she weaves together a tapestry of words."

About the Book

Despite looking forward to a respite from his work with the CIA, Quint Cord is ordered back to Washington by the Director, Gerald Williams, when the President and his family come under attack by unknown forces following his embargo on heavy uranium destined for the country's enemies. When the President's daughter is kidnapped, the Cords move into the White House to assist in locating her. Quint, intuitive and trained in counterterrorism, and Lila, a leading expert in computer hacking, have both earned the President's trust through their commitment and expertise in solving other cases. Despite increased security, threats against the President and his family escalate. It takes a few lucky breaks and a lot of investigation to learn who is behind the carnage. The issue becomes how to stop the perpetrators of the attacks without creating an international incident.

CHAPTER 1

Quint and Lila Cord sat in beach chairs with the waves of the Atlantic lapping their feet. Between them, wedged in the sand and cooled by seawater, sat a bottle of nearly empty Verve Cliquot champagne. It felt good to be able to relax. It felt good to be home, but it felt even better to be safe. The last weeks had been fraught with worry for them both. Working as freelance agents for the CIA was never without its perils. They should have been comfortable with the reality of their careers by now, but neither were. For Quint, having been an agency asset for longer, it was not his knowledge of the dangers which he himself faced that worried him, but a new awareness of the dangers that his new wife faced in her role as one of the world's foremost computer hackers. Quint suspected Gerald Williams, a longtime friend and director of the CIA, would not allow them to luxuriate long in Quint's home on Figure Eight Island on the coast of North Carolina.

He reached back to his dog Code who lay on the wet sand just beyond the water line. Scratching behind Code's ears, Quint soon elicited a low growl of satisfaction from his dog. Despite being in his pet's poor graces after weeks of absence, he seemed to be out of the proverbial doghouse at last.

For more times than he could count, he found himself regretting that he had ever agreed to work for the government. He did not need the money. His authoritarian father had left him a fortune that freed him from the necessity of ever having to work. He could have spent his days in the luxurious beach house he had inherited at his parent's death with his faithful dog and new wife, but Quint was not one to sit idly by while time sifted like beach sand through his fingers. He wanted his life to matter in a productive way by using his God given abilities. He had first come to the attention of the CIA through his skill at code breaking the old-fashioned way…through painstaking analysis of letter and number patterns. That skill was no longer needed, as the age of technology had introduced an entirely new kind of coding. Now, it was his wife Lila that had become the top codebreaker in the world through her computer expertise. His other skills had come to the forefront in this new age. Quint Cord possessed an inquisitive mind that had led him to acquire knowledge in multiple fields. He was inventive, daring, intuitive…a MacGyver type operative. Through training, he had turned his body into a strong, muscular machine that served as backup to his considerable intelligence. He was a nice-looking man, but one that did not stand out. He had a chameleon-like ability to blend into the background that had served him well on numerous occasions.

Lila lifted the bottle of champagne and held it up to the light. "Quint, give me your glass and let's finish this off. Teresa is going to call us in to dinner any minute. She says she is preparing a special feast to welcome us home. She'll kill us if we don't show up on time."

"When I hired Teresa Jones as cook and housekeeper, I had

no idea she would turn into a martinet." Quint laughed at the importance the seemingly unassuming woman had quickly claimed in his household.

"Don't fuss. You know as well as I do, we adore her, and she loves us. Besides, that woman may be the best chef I ever met." Quint laughed and shook his head. "You're right. I suspect we would be lost without Teresa. Either that or trekking into Wilmington or Wrightsville Beach every night to eat."

"Damned right. You know I can't cook. I think opening a can of Vienna sausage and a pack of crackers makes for dinner."

"Oh Lord, spare me." Quint laughed before finishing off his champagne. "Help me get the chairs back to the deck. We have just enough time to stow them and wash off the sand before she will be hollering for us."

Sure enough, no sooner had they deposited the chairs in the underdeck storage area and freshened up, than Teresa's voice rang out to let them know dinner was ready.

Despite repeated invitations to join them at dinner, Teresa refused and ate alone in the kitchen…what she called her turf. At lunch and breakfast, they usually joined her at the kitchen counter, and she would sit down with them for those meals, but never for dinner. Despite days when they might have enjoyed a more casual evening meal, the dining table was always perfectly laid with the linens, fine china, crystal, and the monogramed silver flatware Quint had inherited from his mother. In the center of the table would be an arrangement of whatever flowers Teresa could cultivate in a seaside garden supplemented by arrangements from the local grocery. If one came upon her when she had just finished the table setting, she would be seen standing there admiring her handiwork. Teresa was a proud woman and loved her job with Quint. Her attention to detail, not only in the kitchen but throughout the house, made her an invaluable addition to Quint's home. She had loved Lila from the first time Quint had brought her to his home by the sea, and despite a wary beginning, had warmed to Code. Quint was grateful for that, as it made it much easier to leave his pet behind when called away on a job for the government. He only hoped that the CIA Director would not be calling him anytime soon.

With his honeymoon curtailed when Lila was kidnapped, followed by him and his cohorts in the CIA rescuing her, neither of them wanted anything more than a return to their life on Figure Eight. As if Gerald heard his thoughts, Quint's phone rang. Recognizing the number of the Director's secret line, Quint pushed back from the table.

"I'll take this on the deck, darling."

"Oh, God. Don't tell me that's Gerald Williams," Lila shouted.

Quint gave her a grim smile as he turned to walk out the door and stare at the moonlit sea. He felt Code nudge him as though to say, don't answer. Reaching down he patted his dog's head. Poor Code had learned that calls frequently meant his owner would be leaving him. On the tenth ring, Quint answered, "Gerald, I hope you are calling to welcome me back to the states. We're in need of some serious down time before you put us back in action."

"I'm sorry to have to call, Quint. I know you deserve a break after what you've been through, but this is important. We're going to need you and Lila again." When Quint did not respond, he continued, "I just hung up the phone with President Northrup. His daughter didn't return from school this afternoon. We don't know if she has been abducted or what has happened.

The President has her iPad and computer. As soon I get them, I'm going to have them immediately flown to Wilmington so Lila can hack into her accounts. Her parents don't know the password she may have used. One of our assets in the Wilmington office will pick them up and bring them to your house."

"Dianna's a sixteen-year-old kid. Maybe, she's visiting a friend and just forgot to call. Doesn't she have a Secret Service detail? What did they say?"

Gerald sighed. "Dianna said she was going to the restroom after her last class. How she got away from him without being seen we're not sure. When she didn't come out after fifteen minutes, he called out and then went in. The restroom was empty."

"Any windows she could have gone out?"

"Yeah, but they are pretty high off the floor. It's possible she got out that way as one was open, but it would have been quite a scramble. The only thing we have is a female attendant that exited the restroom shortly after she entered pushing one of those rolling trash cans on wheels. Dianna's Secret Service agent thinks it's possible she could have been hidden in the can. I have someone investigating that now. They are pulling the feed from the video camera in the hallway and dusting down the window and the restroom itself for prints."

"Do you think she could have sneaked off to meet up with a boyfriend?"

"We're interviewing her classmates now to see if she was involved with someone. The President and First Lady are very worried as several threats have been made against him and his family recently. We are waiting to see if they receive a ransom note. The longer we go without knowing what happened, the more dire it looks. I hope I won't need you folks to come to

Washington, but I may have to ask."

"Damn, that's tough. After Lila's kidnapping, I have first-hand experience with the pain they are going through." Quint felt his throat clog with suppressed emotion. Pausing to clear it, he continued, "Sure, send Dianna's stuff on down, and I'll have Lila see what she can do to get into her accounts and dig out a clue for you as to what happened. I hate this for the President. You know you can count on us to do what's needed to get his daughter home safely. Send her birthdate or anything else that might give a clue to her password. That could save time."

"Will do. Give Lila my love…and thank you."

Quint swore under his breath as he walked back into the house. Lila was waiting just inside the door.

"I heard what you said. Let's hope it's a false alarm, and she'll show up soon with a good excuse. When I was about her age, I disappeared to go drinking with my friends. One of them, who was more sober than I, brought me home and hauled me to the front porch where the police found me when they came to file a missing person's report. I thought my parents would ground me forever." Lila shook her head and chuckled at the memory.

"It would be great if you're right. The recent threats the Secret Service has intercepted have me worried, though."

"I do pray Dianna has not been snatched. I remember how terrified I was every minute until you rescued me. I hope she is a smart, tough little cookie. She is going to need to be if someone has grabbed her."

"If she is anything like Clayton Northrup, she's a fighter."

Lila and Quint stared moodily out to sea. Moonlight flickered intermittently on the breakers as the moon broke through the clouds. Neither felt like talking. At ten o'clock, Quint heard the doorbell followed by Teresa's footsteps as she walked to answer it. He looked over at Lila and remarked, "It's going to be a long night, darling."

"For sure. But time is critical. The sooner we can ferret out some clues, the sooner we will have a starting point for finding her. You better believe they are turning Washington upside down as we speak trying to learn anything they can from that end."

"We have some good men in the Agency checking every angle right now. I suspect Gerald has already called Buster Walton to get him on it, too."

*****

Miles to the north in a rural cabin in the Virginia woods, Dianna Northrup slowly opened her eyes. Her head was throbbing with pain. Reaching up she felt a lump on her scalp and a slow ooze. By the dim light in the room, she could see a smear of blood on her fingers. Looking around the small room where she lay on a narrow cot, she noted the rough-sawn wooden walls, a small window that had been nailed over with boards that provided a meager light filtering through the cracks, and a wooden door. Near the cot was a small table with a bottle of water and a roll of toilet paper. Beside them were several protein bars. On the floor under the table was a bucket. With revulsion, she realized two things: whoever had kidnapped her planned to keep her here for some time, and she would have to use the bucket for her bodily waste.

Dianna wiped her brow with the end of her T-shirt. With no air stirring and no air conditioning, the room was oppressively hot. The only prospect for any relief from the heat was the rumble of thunder she could hear in the distance. Looking around the room again, she could see no light, no lantern, and no candle. As night advanced, she would soon be in darkness. Groaning she slowly got up from the cot and made her way to the bucket where she relieved herself. She wrinkled her nose at the smell of her urine and hoped that it would not be left unemptied for long. Next, she went to the table and retrieved the bottle of water and two of the energy bars.

When she returned to her bed, she sat on the edge and slowly ate the bars and drank half of the bottle of water. She was thirsty and wanted to drink all of it, but not knowing when she might be given more, she reserved the rest. She sat the bottle on the floor and lay back on the cot.

She closed her eyes again and tried to think around the pain. Something had gone horribly wrong with the plan to go with her new friend…a recently arrived student to the school…for a girl's shopping trip to the local mall which would be free of the constant hovering presence of her security detail. Barb had assured her they would be fine, and Dianna would be back in time for dinner with her family. Dianna would explain that she had stayed after school to study with her friend. She had not figured out how to explain giving the slip to the security detail. The plan was to meet after class in the restroom and sneak out through the window. By helping one another, they could climb out as they had proved a few days earlier when they had tried it without crawling all the way out. Barb, who had told Dianna she was a year older and had a license, was to park her car close to the back of the school near the restroom window. Dianna had pocketed her allowance that morning and planned to buy the makeup and spaghetti-strap camisole her parents would not allow her to wear. For a little while, she just wanted to feel like any other teenager. She was tired of so many restrictions: never permitted to go anywhere alone, never able to wear the more the daring clothes of her classmates for fear it would reflect badly on her parents, and never allowed to wear anything more than a pale lipstick for formal functions. She could always put on the makeup and the sexy top under her jacket when she got to school. She figured the security detail was so busy looking around for any danger that he barely noticed her. Once she was seated in class with her back to him, she could slip off the jacket and apply the makeup by ducking behind a book. Mr. Atkins always sat at the back of the room beside the door. In each class she had deliberately chosen a seat as far from him as she could get.

Now she wished she had listened to her parents when they warned her that she needed to trust the Secret Service to keep her safe. Joe Adkins, who had been her shadow since her dad's election, was a nice guy and he tried to be inconspicuous as he sensed her resentment at being 'spied on.' She would give anything to see his perpetually worry-lined face at that moment. Dianna regretted that she had caused him trouble. He might even lose his job for letting her be taken and then be replaced by someone she really disliked…that is if she made it out of this mess alive. The thought that she might die was terrifying. Quickly she shoved it from her mind. If she dwelled on that, she would never have the courage to fight back.

Rolling onto her side, she wondered what had happened to Barb. Her friend was waiting in the bathroom when she arrived. She remembered climbing out the window. Then something had hit her on the back of the head, and she could remember nothing more until awakening in this dismal room. She did not want to believe the older and more sophisticated girl had somehow tricked her.

Barbara Rhodes had been so friendly from her first day at the school. Soon they were sitting together at lunch. They would talk with their heads close together so Joe couldn't hear what they were saying. Barb ignored Joe. Sometimes, when he told Dianna she needed to leave, Barb would surreptitiously roll her eyes making Dianna giggle. The other kids were either put off by the Secret Service guy always hanging around, or...impressed by her father's position...assumed she was a snob. Soon Barb was her only close friend. She was even planning to invite her to the White House to the casual suite on the top floor. Dianna thought about calling out to see if Barb was being held in another room. If Barb had escaped, she would tell the agent that someone had hit Dianna in the head and taken her. If they had captured Barb, too, she feared they might kill her so she could not talk.

Dianna was worried about her friend, and she was worried for herself. As night fell, she knew her parents must be frantic. The Secret Service would be searching high and low for a clue for what had happened to her. She could not imagine why someone would take her. After all, her father had always said he would never deal with terrorists, kidnappers, or anyone that tried to extort the country. He loved her, but would his duty to his country override his love for her? If he did nothing to ransom her, would her captors kill her? She felt tears begin to leak from the corners of her eyes. It would feel good to release her terror in a watery flood, but she willed herself not to give in. Her dad was a fighter. He had raised her to be one as well. Now was a true test of her courage and determination to survive whatever she faced. At some point she drifted off to sleep and did not hear someone enter the room, leaving more water, another energy bar, and a fresh bucket.

CHAPTER 2

Lila read over the few notes provided from the President's office when they delivered Dianna's iPad and computer. They were of little to no help beyond the birthdate they included. Intimate details about Dianna Northrup would expedite cracking into her iPad. If that failed, she would try various computer programs she had developed. For that, she decided the best source of information was her mother. Quint listened as she put the call through to the White House. After being routed through different offices there, she had at last been connected to the First Lady. From her, Lila learned details of Dianna's life: the name of her first pet…Snowball, her favorite doll…Miss Kitty, her favorite singer…Gaga, her favorite teacher…Mr. Kirks, her favorite flower…daisies, her favorite book…Harry Potter, and a best friend. Mrs. Northrup was at a loss to provide a friend's name as she knew only that recently Dianna had met someone at school she seemed to really like and had mentioned inviting her to the White House, but the First Lady could not remember if Dianna had told her the girl's name. She explained that Dianna had a tough time adjusting to the Washington fishbowl and felt, both the Secret Service agent hovering over her and her father's position, made kids standoffish. Unlike her classmates, Dianna was not allowed to have any social media platforms. Therefore, they could learn nothing from Facebook or Twitter accounts.

When she hung up, Quint asked, "Did you learn anything helpful?"

"I have a few of the typical things people use for passwords. I am hoping that her iPad screen was cleaned recently. If it was, I'll dust it down for prints and see if I can determine which numerical unlock keys she hit. Then all I must do is work on the various combinations using my algorithm program. I'm going to try that first, then I will try combinations of the things I learned from her mother. I am hoping she used the same password for both the computer and iPad. Have you learned anything more from Gerald?"

"His guys are still working on it. As soon as he has something, he will send me a complete report and we will take it from there. He called Buster Walton and put him on standby."

Lila shook her head and laughed, "That man is a lady-killer mess, but if anyone is going to have our backs, I'm glad he's the one."

"Yeah. He's a pain in the ass sometimes, but invaluable for backup," Quint agreed. "After his help freeing you, he's my friend for life…even if it does tick me off when he ogles you."

Buster Walton was a handsome 6'4" chunk of male brawn. He had a roving eye and a clever mind. Buster had never met a boss. It was that independence of mind that made him a top- notch SEAL, and that same mule-headed streak that saw him leave the SEALS behind and start his own security firm doing clandestine work for the CIA. He followed the rules when it suited him, but mostly went his own way. He loved women but was too foot loose to settle down with one. Quint suspected part of the reason Buster had made no emotional attachments was the same one that had made him reluctant to become involved with Lila. In their line of work, it was dangerous to care too much for someone. It could get you killed. It could also give your enemy leverage over you. Lila's kidnapping had driven that point home to Quint all too well.

While Lila started on the iPad, Quint began compiling a list of known factors. As they learned more, he would add them to the list and start trying to make connections. He watched as Lila dusted powder off the iPad. Blowing it off, she studied the screens carefully for several minutes, before shaking her head and muttering in disgust. Next, she started entering the details that the First Lady had given her into her program. It would sift through millions of combinations that would take forever manually. After long and anxious minutes, nothing turned up.

Quint heard her exhale with exasperation. "It's late, Lila. Let's call it a day. Hopefully, the Secret Service agent assigned to Dianna will get something we can go on when he interviews her classmates tomorrow."

The following morning, they ate a hasty breakfast and were soon sitting in front of their computers hard at work with cooling cups of coffee alongside. From time to time, Lila would utter a curse and when Quint looked her way with raised brow, she would shake her head and continue typing away. After an hour, she leaned back in her chair and took a sip of the now cold coffee.

"Yuk," Lila exclaimed. "I let it get cold."

"Mine, too. I can ask Teresa to make some more if you would like."

"Nah. It doesn't matter."

"You frustrated?"

"You know my program is designed to work so I can track user keystrokes. It doesn't do me a lot of good in this kind of circumstance. I have put in everything I know connected to Dianna, and all I can do now is let my other program try log-on variations. It can do it far quicker than I can. I wish that Secret Service guy would learn something that would help."

Quint glanced at his wristwatch, "I suspect he is asking questions like mad right now. Dianna's school starts at eight. It shouldn't be long before we hear something that might well give us a clue where to begin."

Quint stood up and whistled for Code. "Let's take a walk on the beach. We aren't getting anywhere now anyway. Let your computer programs run and come with me. If Gerald calls, I have my cell phone. As soon as he gives us something, or your program cracks her passcode, we can go back at it."

"We might as well. We're just spinning our wheels at the moment." Lila reached down to scratch Code's ears winning a lick on her hand. "Come on boy."

They watched as Code raced ahead of them to the edge of the waves where foam traced a line on the shore. He was an expert at leaping back when the breakers rolled toward him rarely getting wet above his paws. From time to time, Code veered off to chase sand fiddlers, his favorite beach activity. Quint laughed at Code's antics as he walked along the edge of the incoming tide holding Lila's hand. He treasured the calm moments like this when he could enjoy his wife, the island home his parents had bequeathed to him, and his loyal dog. The sand was soft under their feet as the tide was only just coming in with some of the inrushing water disappearing into the sand while the rest rushed back to sea to join the next incoming breaker. The endless rhythms of the sea soothed him and always refortified his spirit for the next chore the government threw his way. He glanced at

Lila and smiled. Although he rejoiced at having her as his wife, he never ceased fretting that his contract with the CIA and her own celebrated computer expertise put her in danger. Thinking back over the months when he first met, wooed, and then married her, he rued again that he had ever pointed out her rare talent to Gerald Williams. It was frustrating enough when his own activities jeopardized her. It was worse when his job and her own work for the CIA put them in double jeopardy. Unfortunately, there was no going back now. And with the President firmly impressed by their combined skills after exposing an international group determined to seize world domination, he could not bear to let President Northrup down by quietly fading into the sunset of Figure Eight.

A sea gull landed on the edge of the shore ahead sending Code into a barking frenzy. Squawking in alarm, the gull soared airborne to circle above the dog's head. Just out of reach of Code's frantic leaps, the bird's sound switched to what sounded much like laughter at the frustrated dog's efforts. Lila and Quint watched with amusement as Code stuck his nose in the air and stalked after another sand fiddler. Obviously, he was not going to let some bird spoil his dignity.

They had walked almost to the northern end of Figure Eight Island when Quint's phone rang. He pulled it out of his pocket and glanced at the screen. Before answering, he murmured to Lila, "It's Gerald."

"Great. Put him on speaker so I can hear, too."

Quint followed her request before answering, "Hey, Gerald. Do you have something new we can go on? We're pretty much at a standstill here."

Leaning on Quint's shoulder to listen, Lila held her breath as she waited for the answer. She watched her husband's jaw flex as they listened. The news was not good.

Gerald's voice was somber as he replied, "We don't have much to go on from the school so far, but we are a longways from running it all down. Apparently, Dianna befriended a new girl there, name of Barbara Rhodes, who has also vanished. We don't know if she was kidnapped, too, or if she was in on it. Unfortunately, none of the school's information on her checks out. That seems to point to her possible involvement in Dianna's kidnapping. We ran a check on the girl and came up with nothing. The agent assigned to Dianna dusted down both girls' lockers for prints. Dianna's had only hers. The other girl's locker was the same... just her prints. We ran Rhodes' prints through the FBI data base and came up blank."

Quint asked, "I'm curious, you said you had the agent dust down the bathroom window for prints? Did he find the girls' prints on the outside window?"

"Damn. I cannot believe I forgot to ask Agent Adkins if he did that. He said he dusted the inside of the windowsill, and he did find both of their prints there. The latch had just Dianna's friend's prints. I'm going to ask him to dust the outside as well, if he has not already done so."

"Let us know what he finds."

"I'll do it. We're asking around the neighborhood to see if anyone saw anything. The kids say the Rhodes girl had a car, a Honda, gray, late model, maybe two-door. We are checking on all registrations in the entire D.C. area that match that description. I also have the school pulling security camera footage to see if someone can identify anyone that was in the school at the time that was not either a student or on staff. They will also pull footage with the Rhodes girl on it."

"Check to see if the woman with the rolling trashcan is a recent hire. If so, it would be good to run that to the ground to see if there is anything there. Also, I'd like to know if she is still working at the school."

"Good points, Quint. If my guys aren't already on it, I'll put a bug in their ears. In the meantime, as soon as I get the security camera feed, I will post it so you and Lila can go through it. My agents will be doing the same. Between the different sets of eyes, hopefully someone will spot something. When you said y'all are pretty much at a standstill, I assume Lila did not yet break into Dianna's computer and iPad?"

"Hi, Gerald. I'm listening in on the call," Lila replied. "I tried all of the combinations using the information the First Lady provided, but nothing worked. I have my computer program running through combinations now. We're on the beach taking a break in hopes the computer has come up with the password by the time we go back. If so, I'll immediately go through her emails and texts to see what I can produce."

"If you are unable to get in, I will contact Apple to see if they will get into the iPad for us. Normally they aren't easy to work with, but with the President's daughter's life at stake, maybe they will be a little more amenable."

"That's a slow process as you know. I'm hoping I can crack it myself, so we don't lose any more time than necessary."

"Well, Lila, if anyone can do it, it's you," Gerald answered. "You guys should have the video feed when you get back to the house. If you learn anything, no matter how trivial, let me know. In the meantime, I am going to call Adkins again to see if he dusted the exterior of the building. I'll be in touch soon."

Quint responded, "Thanks, Gerald."

When they ended the call with the CIA Director, they turned wordlessly to retrace their steps to the house. Code was not happy their walk was cut short as he had just found a new sand fiddler to torment. He stood in the shallows barking at their backs as he scratched madly after the rapidly disappearing crab. Quint whistled without turning. Giving up the sand fiddler as a lost cause, Code grumbled in his throat, but reluctantly followed. When they reached the house, they immediately went to their computers. Lila's program was still spinning, so they settled in front of Quint's screen and downloaded the security camera video Gerald had sent. Both grabbed pens and note pads as the video began playing. With the start time at 7 a.m., they were in for a long session before arriving at the afterschool visit when Dianna went to the restroom and disappeared.

They were only two hours into the scanning when the phone rang again. Glancing at the screen, Quint announced, "It's Gerald. Let's hope he has something new for us to go on."

"Yeah, Gerald. What's up?"

"You are not going to believe this crap. The President's staff just called to say the White House computers have been shut down. They were attacked by ransom ware. At this point we don't know what they are after in the way of ransom. But with the President's daughter kidnapped and now the hack, we have some serious enemy out there."

"It sure looks like it. What do you want us to do? Were any other government systems compromised?"

"No, just the White House. I'm pulling Lila to chase down the hackers. I want you to keep working on the kidnapping. I will send you both everything we have from here that might help. Tell

Lila to expect the White House encrypted info, IP address, passcodes, etc. Hopefully, she will be able to track it back to the ransom ware, bypass it, and regain control. We are working now to shut down any potentially compromised critical websites. I don't have to tell you how disastrous this could be for national security."

CHAPTER 3

Dianna was awakened the next morning by the sensation of someone standing over her. She pretended to sleep for another few seconds while she gathered the courage to open her eyes and face whatever awaited her. The sight that greeted her was both a glad one and one that made her even more fearful at the same time.

Dianna sat up and erupted with a torrent of words, "Barb, they took you, too! I am so sorry you are in this mess, but I'm so glad you are alive. When I didn't see you, I was afraid they might have killed you. When did they put you in here with me? Are you alright? Do you have any idea why we were kidnapped?"

Lena, the girl Dianna knew as Barb, laughed derisively, "You are so damned gullible. We set you up and you didn't have a clue. Poor little President's daughter just wanted a friend. Well, you picked the wrong one, little girl."

Dianna was stunned by the change in this girl she had thought was her friend and someone she thought she could trust. She studied Barb carefully noting the changes. The person standing in front of her was much older looking than she had appeared at school. Her hair was different both in color and cut. Her face was no longer open and friendly, but cold and closed. "You're right, Barb. I'll hand it to you…you're a good actress. So, why kidnap me?"

"You're the President's daughter. The folks I work for want something from him and you are their ticket for getting it. You do what we tell you, and we will let you go. If you don't, it won't be pleasant."

"You don't know my father. I may be his daughter, but he has stated publicly over and over that he will not be held hostage by terrorists, unfriendly countries, or anyone else. Furthermore, why should I believe you will let me go when I can identify you. He will not negotiate, trust me."

"That may be, but no one took his daughter before. Not just his daughter, but his only child."

"Who are you, Barb? Is that even your real name?"

"All of that is irrelevant." For a second or two she looked uneasy, before continuing, "We need a video recording of you reading a prepared statement for your father. All you need to do is read it just as it is written. That will also assure him that you have not been harmed. Surely you want your parents to have that reassurance."

Dianna reminded herself that she was her father's daughter. He would not go down without a fight and neither would she. "That depends on that statement. I don't plan to make it easy for you to kill me. Furthermore, the Secret Service will know you disappeared when I did, and they will be looking for you, too. What makes you think the people you are working for will risk you being caught and blabbing. They'll probably kill you, too."

"Stop it. I told you if you cooperate you will go free." Barb did not hide her annoyance nor a momentary flicker of fear in her eyes. "There is a camera set up in the other room. On the desk is the paper you are to read. Add nothing. Just read it. Now, get up and follow me." Dianna stared at her for a long moment before she complied. If nothing else, perhaps the appearance of the other room might give her a clue as to a possible escape route. As for reading the statement for her father, she would decide after she had read what it said.

The outer room resembled the one in which she was imprisoned: rough-hewn wooden walls, a haphazardly boarded-over window, and what appeared to be an exterior door judging from the light leaking in around the edges. In the center of the room was a desk with a camera situated in front of it. No one else was there. Obviously, Barb herself would be running the recording.

Dianna walked over to the desk and sat in the chair facing the camera. She picked up the paper and silently read what it said: *"If you want to see your daughter alive, you will follow the directives we send you. By now your computer systems will have been compromised and we will send you our demands on the White House email which we programmed to receive messages both to and from you. When you comply with all we ask, we will release control of the White House computer system and return your daughter to you. As you can see, she is unharmed. If you want her to remain that way, do what we say."*

Dianna placed the paper back on the desk. She kept her head down as she thought of what she wanted to say to Barb. She planned some demands of her own. Whether she would get them remained to be seen. But she would try.

Barb interrupted her thoughts, "Get on with it!" she snapped. Dianna looked up and glared at the girl she had thought was her friend.

"No. If you want me to read this, then I want something in return. You need to give me better food than snack bars, and I want to go outside for some fresh air once a day."

"I don't have the authority to promise you that. Stop stalling and read."

"So, call someone that has the authority. Until I get what I want, you don't get what you want."

"You're turning into a real bitch, Miss President's Daughter." Barb growled, "Stay there and don't try anything. I'll be right back."

Dianna watched as Barb opened the door. In the moment before the door slammed shut, she could see nothing but woods outside the cabin. Quickly, she jumped from her seat and ran to the window to peep between the boards. In the opening she could see Barb's car and behind that an unpaved road that led into the woods. On the left side was what she took to be a creek as she could hear the murmur of running water. If she could find a way to escape, she could follow the creek until she came to a road. Satisfied she could learn nothing more, she hurried back to the chair behind the desk. She was sitting there staring at the door when it opened, and Barb walked back in.

"I'll bring you a meal when I return but you are not going to be allowed to go outside. I'll bring you a meal each day while you are here...just one. Otherwise, if you're hungry, you have the protein bars. That's the best I can do for you."

"Thank you. When will you be back with something to eat?"

"Read the statement. After you have done that, I can go. I'll be back tonight with food."

"Why should I trust you?"

Barb shrugged her shoulders, "Suit yourself. But I promise you if you do not read that statement, you will have a visit from someone that is going to quickly make your life both difficult and very painful."

Dianna did not respond immediately as she sat considering her options. There were few. Reluctantly Dianna picked up the paper and said, "Let's get on with this then."

When Barb had finished recording the statement that Dianna read, she ordered her to return to the inner room. Dianna shrugged her shoulders without comment and walked into the room as ordered. Standing just inside the door, she heard the key turn in the lock and moments later the sound of a car engine. In the corner of the room, she spotted the backpack that she had been carrying when she was taken. At the sight of it, her heart soared. Inside was the stylus used in her printmaking class. Made of steel, it was a formidable weapon with sharp points on each end. She wondered if it also might be a tool she could use to pry loose the boards on the window. If she could get even two off, she could break the window and climb out. If that did not work, when Barb brought the promised food, she would attack her and escape in Barb's car. The thought of harming the girl she had thought a friend caused a momentary qualm, but she quickly brushed the thought aside. She was in a fight for her life and that was the only thing she needed to consider.

She wasted no time digging the stylus from the bottom of her backpack and attacking the lock on the door. When it refused to budge despite numerous probes with the stylus, she turned her attention to the boards on the window. Try as she might, she could not get enough leverage on the stylus to make any progress. After two hours, she sat down on the floor and sobbed with frustration. Drying her tears, she got up and retrieved one of the protein bars and the bottle of water. After eating her meagre lunch, she felt some better and resolved to try again.

By dusk, she had managed to pry the board up by only a

quarter of an inch. If she could just get one end loose, she could then leverage the board away from the window frame and then use that board to help pry out the others. It would take most of the following day. Dianna chuckled to herself. It wasn't as though she had anything else to do. Hiding the tool under the scant mattress on her cot, Dianna sat down and awaited the promised meal. Well after nightfall, she heard a car outside the cabin followed by footsteps approaching the cabin. She prayed it was Barb and not someone even more sinister.

She turned toward the sound of the lock turning, followed by the opening of the door. Barb stood silhouette in the doorframe backlit by the light in the outer room.

"I hope you brought food. I'm starving. I also hope you brought a candle or something to see by as it is difficult to eat in the dark."

Barb sat the bag of food on the bed and retrieved the bucket of waste from the corner. She wrinkled her nose as she lifted it. "I'll leave the door open so you can see by the light in the other room. I'll be dumping this just outside the door, so don't try anything. I warn you if you do, I will not hesitate to kill you."

"You know, Barb, you could have been a nice person. Instead, you are someone I cannot imagine anyone liking. I don't know what made you do something like this, but I feel sorry for you."

"Save your pity for yourself, Dianna. You may need it before this is all over." Barb spun on her heel and stalked out of the cabin with the bucket as Dianna opened the bag and drew out a McDonald's double cheese hamburger, fries, and a soft drink.

She hungrily bit into the burger and chewed happily. At least she had achieved one small thing for herself.

When Barb returned, Dianna paused in chewing to comment,

"It's hot in here and I smell. It's bad enough that I must wear the same clothes every day, but not even to be able to bathe makes it worse. Do you think I could have some soap and bathwater?"

"Aren't you the spoiled one…always demanding. You need to understand you are in the position to demand nothing. I'm bringing you food and emptying your shit. Don't expect me to become your personal servant."

"No problem. It doesn't hurt to ask."

Barb did not reply. She glanced around the room before leaving Dianna to finish her meal in the dark. When she had finished eating, Dianna put the trash back in the bag, used the toilet and prepared for bed. Removing her jeans and shirt, she laid them at the foot of the bunk and climbed under the thin sheet more for modesty than anything as the room was hot. Lying there she could not help thinking about her parents and how worried they must be since her abduction. She glanced at her watch. It was eight at night. She had been taken the day before at three o'clock making nearly thirty hours that she had been held. She was sorry that she had often been sulky and obstinate about the restrictions on her necessitated by her father's office. Sleep refused to come no matter how many sheep she counted.

Sitting up on her cot, she swatted at a mosquito that persisted in buzzing around her head. When that did not drive the pest away, she pulled the sheet over her head teepee fashion and continued mulling what she had learned that day. If she began early the next morning, she should be able to finish loosening the lower board and would use it as a lever to remove the remaining ones. She remembered watching her former friend glancing around the room to make sure it was undisturbed when she brought the food. If she loosened the boards and Barb returned the next day before she escaped, Barb would know what she was up to. If Barb did not return before nightfall she might succeed in escaping.

Her biggest fear was that Barb, or another, would come before she could gain her freedom. If that were the case, her only recourse would be to use the stylus as a weapon. She hated even imagining that scenario and quickly turned her mind from the idea of doing murder. If she had to kill to save herself, she had no choice. But could she live with the idea of having taken another person's life, especially Barb's...who she reminded herself had not really been her friend.

Lying down with the cover over her head as protection from the annoying mosquito, she forced herself to relax. If she were to escape her prison, she needed to rest and be ready to pry the window boards loose, climb out, and face whatever awaited beyond.

Suddenly it dawned on her that the food she had eaten had been slightly warm. There must be a McDonald's nearby and that meant civilization. Although the food was warm, the town could still be miles away. She dared not take the road that led from the cabin and that meant she would have to make her way through the woods.

The night noises of the forest sounded as loud as thunder to ears accustomed to the well-insulated quietness of her room in the White House. As a last resort she pulled the pillow over her head and turned to her side. Even if she could not sleep, she had to rest.

When the first light of dawn crept through the cracks in the boarded-up window, Dianna pulled on her clothes. She ate one of the protein bars and washed it down with water. That done she relieved her bladder. Reaching under her mattress, she felt for the stylus. She could not afford to waste daylight as she had no idea how long it would take to loosen enough boards to break the window and climb out.

This was it. Once she had those boards off, she had to leave and fast. Before beginning on the board, she added the bottle of water and two remaining protein bars to the contents. For a moment she considered the sweater that was lying on the floor and that she always kept inside. If she were forced to spend the night in the woods, it might come in handy. She decided to add it to the bag. Although Barb had removed her phone from her jeans, she had not thought to take the special key fob that allowed her access to the private entry to the White House. Either Barb did not realize its value, or she had overlooked it. Dianna added that to her bag and sat it beside the window. Then she began trying to pry the board enough that she could wrest it loose.

Chapter 4

Quint listened with growing irritation as Gerald Williams explained that President Northrup wanted Lila and him to relocate to Washington to work on his daughter's kidnapping. "Damn Gerald, we have hardly had time to get back home and catch up on things here. My dog was growling at me like I was some kind of stranger. I have a stack of bills and paperwork to go through. We can work from here just fine."

"After you broke the Alliance for Global Union case, the President thinks you two hung the moon. The man's worried sick. Humor him. If one of my sons had been taken, I cannot imagine how frantic I would be. It doesn't help that the President has taken a hard line with terrorists. He doesn't know how to backdown and still maintain the integrity of his word. If he doesn't back down and Dianna is harmed, the First Lady is going to come close to killing him. We will set you up in an office in the White House where you will have close contact and immediate information on everything that happens. The President has already ordered a space cleaned out for you to use as an office and a suite. You won't find a nicer accommodation than that."

"I'll ask Lila. If we come, I'm bringing my dog."

Gerald laughed, "If Code were mine, I would probably do the same thing. You two talk it over and get back to me ASAP. Time is critical. I don't have to tell you that."

"Yeah. I know that well. Later." Quint ended the call and turned to Lila. "You heard?"

"Yeah. We might as well go pack. When the President orders us, we have no choice do we?"

In the White House, Clayton Northrup was not meeting with the same agreement from his wife.

Mary Northrup was in tears. Not only was she terrified for her daughter, but now she looked at her husband as someone she did not know, and at that moment didn't particularly like. Raising her head, she glared at him, "Why don't you give her kidnappers what they want so they will release our daughter?"

"Mary, I have explained it all. You know I love our child as much as you do, and I want her safely home more than anything. If I were just any father, it would be easy. But I'm not. As President, my priority is the country I swore to serve. When I ran for office I explained to you what it would entail if I won. You agreed…"

"Yes, but you never said a damned thing about doing nothing if our daughter were to be kidnapped? I suppose it would have been the same thing if they had taken me, too."

"That's not fair. You both mean the world to me. If I give them what they are demanding, we will be at the mercy of every enemy government and terrorist group in the world. That is the first problem. The second is what they are demanding. They want me to back down on the Chinese-Russian armament deal with North Korea and Iran and the sanctions I placed on all four countries. We cannot allow North Korea and Iran to join in a nuclear agreement with China and Russia. The entire world would be in jeopardy. It is especially worrisome with the growing military power of an increasingly aggressive China."

"If you do nothing, they will kill our only child. Could you really live with yourself if that happened? Could you forgive yourself? I don't know if I could."

Clayton's face looked as though he had aged ten years since Dianna was taken and his heart was breaking. If they lost Dianna, he knew his wife would hate him. He wanted to tell his wife what she wanted to hear, not just for her, but for his daughter and himself. He struggled to stop the tears welling in his eyes. Clearing his throat, he gathered his wife in his arms. "Darling, we are doing everything we can to discover who has her and to get her back. Remember, if Quint Cord and Buster Walton were able to recover Quint's wife, they can find Dianna, too. Not only that, but Lila Cord is the best there is at hacking into computer systems. Between the three of them and our national security agencies, we are going to find the bastards that did this. I have everyone I can working on this. We will get our daughter back. Just have faith, Mary, and trust me to do everything I can short of giving in."

Mary Northrup looked into her husband's eyes. Her voice was hard as she said, "See that you get her back...alive and unharmed. I don't care how you do it, just do it."

Five minutes later, Clayton Northrup sat in his chair in the Oval Office with his arms crossed on the desk. Resting his head on, his arms he allowed the memory of his days before the Presidency to wash over him. He envisioned Mary, twenty years younger and dressed in an elegantly simple gown as she walked down the aisle to where he stood waiting. How he had managed to win the hand of the daughter of the top lawyer in the law firm where he was the most junior still amazed him. With her beauty and personality, she could have had her pick of beaux, but she had seen something in him. She had believed in him more than he believed in himself, and it was that assurance that had led him to the most powerful position in the world. He recalled the day he first held their child in his arms. He was so afraid of dropping the warm little bundle, and for the first time he became truly aware of the awesome responsibility of fatherhood. Again, Mary had smiled reassuringly as she watched his trepidation. There were so many good memories as he rose in the firm and earned enough to buy their first home, first new car, and even enroll Dianna in an elite private school. Had he never agreed to run for his first office in the Senate, he would still have had a comfortable and prosperous life. If he had not won the Presidency, his daughter would be like any other teenager enjoying all the things that period of life brings. As it was, his decision to serve his country jeopardized everything he loved in his personal life. He wondered if life would ever return to the simple joy of waking up with his wife curled up beside him and his daughter sleeping peacefully down the hall.

It was a moment before he noted the persistent buzzing of the phone on his desk that signaled his assistant was trying to reach him. Picking up the receiver and praying for no bad news, he awaited whatever new problem had arisen. "Sir, the Cords are here along with Mr. Walton."

"Thank you. Please show them in."

The President arose when they entered and walked around his desk to shake their hands. "Thank you so much for coming. As you can imagine, the First Lady and I are worried sick. Take a seat and I will share with you the crux of the problem."

They all took seats while the President walked back and sat behind his desk. Swiping his hand across his face, he began, "It's probable the Russians...in collusion with China, North Korea, and Iran...are behind this. The kidnappers posted a recording of my daughter along with a list of their ransom demands on the White House network servers they have compromised by hacking into and freezing access to all the accounts. I think you are aware of that, Lila; and I am counting on you to ascertain the source of the hacking and block them at the source. We had the CIA create another server that is secure so far. You will have access to that and to the hacked account."

Lila nodded her understanding as he continued, 'Quint and Buster, I need you to find my daughter. They have backed me into a corner. I dare not give the hackers what these rogue nations want, but if I don't, they have promised to kill my daughter. It would be easy if I could put one life over the good of the country, but as Commander in Chief, I don't have that luxury...not even for my own daughter."

Quint gestured to Buster who signaled him to respond, "Mr. President, we are aware of the difficulty of this situation, both internationally and personally. We assure you we will do everything we can to find Dianna and return her safely to you. Please see that the recording they sent you is available for us to view."

"We have been unable to copy or forward it. My secretary will arrange for you to view it on the White House site."

"Thank you. We hope we can derive some clues from the recording," Buster explained.

"I am counting on you three. I have told Director Williams to provide you with whatever resources you need to get the job done. I have also arranged for you to stay in the guest rooms as the personal guests of my wife and me. There is a bedroom, bath, closets, and what was an adjoining bedroom has been converted into a sitting room. You should be comfortable there, and since there are no other guests on the floor you will have some privacy. If you have any dietary restrictions or preferences, please let my assistant know. I have arranged for someone to take you to your rooms and get you settled. Quint, you will find your dog is already in the suite assigned to you."

"We are honored, Mr. President."

"Fine, now let's all get busy." Northrup stood and leaned across his desk to shake their hands in dismissal. "Good luck!"

Once they had settled in their rooms, Mark Abrams, the aide that was their appointed liaison, returned to lead them to their office in the basement of the White House. He walked them to an elevator and waited for them to enter. He punched in a code, and the elevator car began to descend. He chuckled before commenting, "You don't know how privileged you are to be in this area. Obviously, the President thinks you are pretty special to be given guest rooms and access here."

When the elevator car stopped and the doors slid open, Quint, Lila, and Buster looked around at the austere walls that were in stark contrast to the upper levels of the White House. Here it was all business. Adams beckoned them to follow him as he led them down a hallway and stopped in front of a door. Before entry, he logged each of them in via pupil telemetry. All future access to the locked space would require peering into the sensor for pupil recognition whereby the office door would be automatically unlocked. They followed him into the windowless room full of blinking lights and lit computer screens that turned it into perpetual twilight. He explained the access code that cleared them to use the computers. Lila queried him about the programs downloaded on the machines and requested permission to temporarily download those she had developed. Abrams hesitated before complying with a request that he had not previously faced. The woman's reputation preceded her, and if the President wanted her help, he had little choice but to give her whatever exceptions she needed. He nodded agreement, before continuing with protocol.

Lila, as the primary user of the facility, intently followed his words. When Adams paused, she queried, "According to the President, the White House server has been compromised by the hack. Are the ones I am to use on the new server.?"

"Yes. These were not compromised. We immediately changed protocol on these to a new IP address. The last time we checked, the ones in this room were not compromised."

"When was that?"

"Two hours ago."

"I will re-verify before I attempt to do anything else. Make sure we stay separate from all other operating systems. I need this one to remain autonomous."

"No problem. Over here is the computer on the server that has been compromised. Give me a moment while I will pull up the recording of Dianna made by the kidnappers. You can leave it running. Just shake the mouse to keep it on the screen."

The four of them pulled up chairs and sat in front of the screen. A deceptively calm Dianna read through the prepared script. After that, a faceless voice stated the terms of her release. Buster and Quint looked at each other. They both had the same thought: the chances of recovering the President's daughter were slim to none with a President that had made it a hallmark of his office not to compromise with terrorists.

Quint silently signaled Buster once Mark Abrams had left the three of them alone to acquaint themselves with the facility. Quint spoke, "Lila, you don't need us here. We're going to make a visit to Gerald Williams and go over the files. We need to know everything they have gathered so far to see if we can find any clues to Dianna's kidnappers and where they might have taken her."

"That's fine. I'll see you upstairs later." Quint could see Lila was so intent on logging onto the computers and setting up her own system, she barely gave them a glance.

Leaning over, he kissed the top of her head and said, "Love you, babe."

The first malware group Lila checked was the Evil Corp who had used a Dridex malware toolkit to hack into dozens of U.S. sites. After it was busted by the Department of Justice in 2019 and two of the members were indicted, the group switched to WastedLocker. Their attacks classically began with hacking sign-in passwords, followed by a false notice of software update. When the user logged on to the update, a JavaScript-based framework known as SocGholish took over the system, disabled Windows, and using the Windows Sysinternals PsExec tool, encrypted data, and deleted shadow volumes containing file backups. Lila suspected that was the culprit as no one had yet been able to break through their firewall. She was determined she would. The group was a danger to every computer system in every government, company, and private household in an increasingly networked world. Not only must they be stopped from a security standpoint, but she was determined to track them and hold them 'ransom' until Dianna was released. How she would do that, she had not figured out, but she would. She would not quit until she had. The question would be what she could hold over them as ransom. Perhaps, the President or Gerald Williams could steer her in the right direction. She had never been so deeply emmeshed in the government logistics and politics, thus had little concept of how to approach what could well be a political dilemma with major repercussions if she created some counter threat to the terrorists.

In her mind she found herself telling Dianna to be brave and hold on. No one realized better than Lila the terrible fear of having been taken…of wondering if she would live through the ordeal. Thanks to Quint, Buster, and the CIA agents who worked with them, she had been rescued. This time she would be a part of the rescue team.

CHAPTER 5

Dianna threw the sheet off her body the moment the light of dawn crept through the cracks between the boards over the window. She was soon dressed. After eating a protein bar and drinking some water, she retrieved the stylus from beneath her mattress. She walked over to the door and leaned her ear against it to listen. She heard nothing from the other room. The only sound to reach her was from the exterior of the cabin where birds were chirping-in the new day. The sounds gave a sense of peace beyond her prison. If she could only reach that freedom, she swore never to take things for granted again…her parents, a nice bath, clean clothes, food, water whenever she needed it, and a toilet. The mundane things that had comprised her daily life she had never thought about or appreciated. They had all been taken for granted.

Shrugging her shoulders to shake off all thoughts except the necessity to free herself before Barb returned, Dianna pried on the board she had begun to loosen the day before. The screech of the nails slowly releasing their hold on the wood sounded loud in her ears. Stopping, she listened again at the door. Hearing nothing, she resumed her work. After an hour of unrelenting effort one end was free. Using that for leverage, she pried the other end loose. There was no turning back now. Repeating the procedure, in another hour she freed the second board. The opening now looked large enough to wiggle through. Dianna lugged the table over to the window, sat her backpack on it and placed the stylus inside. It was her only weapon should she need one. She added the bottle of water and the extra protein bar. She then returned to the bed where she snatched off the sheet and balled it around her fist to protect her hand. Thus prepared, she slammed her hand repeatedly into the window until it was free of glass. Brushing away the glass, she nodded her head. It was time to go.

First, she dropped her backpack onto the ground below the window. Then contorting her body so she could go out legs first she worked herself out the window using the table to push against. Dianna dropped to the ground and took a deep breath and picked up her backpack. The only sounds were those of the forest and the distant murmur of a stream. She headed into the woods in the direction of the sound of the water. She ran as though a thousand ghouls were at her back in fear that her abductors would return and catch her. If that should happen, she doubted they would allow her to live. No matter what hardship the forest presented she had no choice but to flee until she could find safe haven.

Twenty minutes later Dianna reached the brook and paused to catch her breath. Sitting on a mossy mound, she considered removing her tennis shoes and putting them in her backpack but figured she would make better time shod. Gingerly she stepped into the stream and began to walk the rocky bed toward what she hoped would be civilization. The water was cool, but not cold. The biggest discomfort was the occasional misstep that caused her to slip. Ignoring the pain caused by a slight twist of her ankle, she kept wading. She did not know how far she had walked when the sound of distant gunshots caused her to turn her head. Shaking with fear, she climbed out of the stream and onto the muddy bank. She listened in frozen terror. When she heard nothing more, she again waded back into the stream and resumed walking. Trying to remember the direction she had traveled she deduced the shots had come from the general direction of the cabin.

*****

Barb arrived early at the cabin with orders to tape several videos of Dianna saying she was unharmed. She hated doing it. The message was clear. Dianna could be eliminated at will, but they would still have the videos as leverage while the President stalled on complying with demands. If they were willing to kidnap and then kill the President's daughter, they would not hesitate to kill her, as well. She knew her contact and his boss. They were ruthless.

She entered the cabin and unlocked the door to the room where Dianna was being held. When she swung the door open, she stared in shock at the empty room. The boards lying on the floor and the broken window said it all. Their hostage was gone. There would be no more videos unless she could find her.

Barb tore out of the cabin in a panic. Hopefully, Dianna had not gone far, and she would be able to bring her back and take the videos. She had no idea in which direction to go. Stopping for a moment she considered the options. The most logical and the easiest escape was the road. Retracing the pathway on which she had arrived, this time on foot, she began walking down the road checking the bushes on either side as she went. Periodically she stopped to listen. Only the sounds of the forest came back to her. After an hour, she was tired, scratched from the brambles… and despite the heat, the perspiration on her brow was the cold sweat of fear. She had not signed up for this. Originally, she had been told to befriend Dianna and then to take her to the cabin for a couple of days until the kidnappers' demands were met. She was stupid to believe they would let the girl go unharmed. She should have known it was not going to be a simple hostage taking. These were not nice people that had hired her.

Barb considered calling for her but was afraid that would only drive Dianna farther away if she heard her shouts. Overwhelmed with despair, she turned back towards the cabin. There were no tracks to indicate she had come this way. When she reached the cabin, she debated getting in the car and running...but where? Her flurry of random thoughts was interrupted by the buzz of her phone. Looking down at the screen, she recognized the number. The phone stopped ringing while she stared at it only to start again a few seconds later. Sighing, Barb answered.

The man she knew as Ivan asked, "Why have you not sent the videos we need? You should have done them by now."

Barb's voice was almost a whisper when she replied, "She's escaped. I've tried to find her. I can't."

"I see," his voice was tight with controlled anger. "Stay there and wipe down the cabin. We don't want to leave any fingerprints that would indicate that either of you were there. You will find Clorox and rags in the cabinet in the front room. I will be there shortly, and we'll look for her together."

"Okay." Barb stuffed her phone back in her jeans.

She stood still and thought. She could leave and with a thirty-minute head start she could perhaps escape, but for how long could she elude them? The other option was to do as she had been ordered and wait for Ivan to arrive. He did not sound as though she was in trouble, and he did say he would come and help her find Dianna. Reassuring herself she had nothing to fear, she began wiping down the cabin as ordered. She had just finished when she heard his tires on the dirt road leading in. Barb stowed the cleaning materials and walked to the open door of the cabin to await Ivan.

He opened the door of his car and got out. His voice terse, he barked, "Come on. We're going to start looking."

"I checked the road and saw no sign of her there."

"I planned to start in the woods anyway." He beckoned her to follow him as he walked around the wooded perimeter of the cabin. He stopped from time to time to check the ground and surrounding bushes looking for some indication of the route she had taken. Halfway around the cabin, he stopped and peered closely at the ground and then at a broken twig on a nearby bush. Checking the twig, he could see that it was a fresh break. "Come on. She went into the woods here."

Barb followed him into the woods kicking herself for not checking the perimeter as he had done. If she had done so, she might have been able to catch Dianna before she went too far. As it was, she could only hope that Dianna was going slowly so they could catch her before she reached help. If they did not find her, she knew she would be in terrible trouble. Ivan kept a rapid pace, forcing her to struggle to get through the brambles and keep up. She ruefully acknowledged her shorts were far more an impediment than his long pants. They had gone for perhaps a half mile into the woods when they reached a shallow ravine. Ivan stopped and ordered her to come closer. A sinking feeling in her gut told her she had made a terrible mistake in waiting for him. When she came near, he grabbed her arm and shoved her into the ravine. She landed face down at the bottom, scratched and winded from panic, but otherwise unharmed. Struggling to rise, the last thing she heard was the click of a gun as Ivan pulled back the hammer. Barb fell forward into the rotted leaves that lined the depression. Ivan scrambled down the bank and checked the side of her neck for a pulse. Finding only a very faint one and noting the copious bleeding, he assumed she would be dead before long. Next, he checked her pockets for her phone but did not find it. That meant he would have to go back to the cabin and search for the phone. Ivan began pulling leaves over her body to conceal it from any immediate eyes. When he was satisfied that the body was sufficiently covered to prevent discovery except through the most thorough of searches, he stood up and looked around him. After a few days, the forest predators would remove any identifying features. He smiled. With false papers and an illegal entry through Canada, she would never be identified even if her body were discovered. He left her with no more concern than he would have shown a bag of garbage.

Trying to put himself in the fleeing girl's mind, he studied the surrounding forest for any clues of where she might have run. He could hear the stream gurgling over roots and rocks as it made its way downhill. It was something to follow until it reached a bigger creek or river and then flowed onward to civilization. Were he the one running, he would follow the stream. The girl had already proven herself intelligent enough to escape the cabin, so she had likely reached the same conclusion. Scrambling back up the embankment, he followed the noise of the running water. From time to time, he searched laterally to see if he could discern her actual path downward. After fifteen minutes, Ivan found a broken branch that appeared to be fresh as sap still oozed from the break. Again, he paused and looked around. Immediately in front of where he stood was a steep escarpment of sharp rock formations. Deciding she would have skirted that, he walked first to the right and finding nothing to indicate she had taken that detour, he began to search the left side. Midway down, he spied a depression that could only have been left by a tennis shoe or some similar footwear judging by the impression left in the mud. Confident he was on the right path, he hurriedly continued to descend to the bank of the stream.

When Ivan reached the bank, he again paused to study the terrain. Swiveling around to check in both directions, his foot slipped on the mud, and he slid into the water up to his left ankle. Cursing vehemently, he staggered to get his balance and pull his foot out. Clambering back up the bank to a fallen log, he sat down, untied his laces, and removed the wet sock and tossed it aside. He dug into his trouser pocket and retrieved a handkerchief which he used to dry out the inside of his shoe. Next, he scrubbed as much of the mud from the exterior as he could before thoughtlessly tossing the soiled handkerchief to the ground in disgust. With that done, he stood and began to walk along the edge of the stream keeping well back from the muddy verge. His surmise of the direction the girl had taken paid off when he spied a footprint in the mud just ahead. At that point, the track disappeared into the water. Sighing with disgust, Ivan retreated up to the bank, and found a mossy spot to sit. He considered removing his shoes, but the thought of walking on rocks and hidden debris was unappealing. He stood and studied the stream for a moment. Gingerly he stepped into the water. He had not gone three steps when his leather soled shoes caused him to lose his footing on a moss-covered rock. The next thing he knew he was sitting on the bed of the stream as the water parted to rush around him. He was wet to his waist and thoroughly angry at the aggravation the little bitch was causing him. He pulled his gun from his pocket and shook it to clear water from the barrel. Shoving it back in his pocket, Ivan removed his shoes and using his laces he tied them together and hung them around his neck. He then began wading down the stream stepping gingerly from rock to rock. From time to time, he cursed as he stepped on a sharp rock. Never one to enjoy going barefoot, his feet were tender, and the water made them more so. The girl was lucky to be wearing tennis shoes and not leather ones like his.

Ivan continued walking down the stream for an hour. He constantly paused to check both banks to make sure she had not left the stream. Sweat poured into his eyes from the exertion. Not having a handkerchief any longer, he resorted to wiping the sweat from his forehead onto his shirt sleeves. The longer he tracked Diana, the angrier he became. He swore he would punish the bitch before eventually killing her. He enjoyed rape, but he would make sure she would not. Maybe he would shoot her in both kneecaps first. After he had raped her, he would take pleasure in killing the girl. He smiled to himself as he stopped to wipe his forehead again. He reminded himself that first they needed a series of videos of her saying she was unharmed and being well treated. After that, she was a liability.

After an hour of careful tracking, he was about ready to call it quits when he espied footprints on the left bank. Gingerly stepping on rocks to reach the bank, he bent to study the impressions. The prints were hers. Even though she was traveling faster, wearing his shoes he should be able to catch up. He wasted no time sitting down and putting his shoes on.

Standing up in his still wet shoes, he followed the direction the footprint indicated. Thirty minutes later he felt the beginnings of blisters on his sockless left heel, a result of the wet leather without a sock to cushion them and with his feet softened from long exposure in the water. Every step became an agony causing him to slow unconsciously. He considered removing his shoes and going barefoot, but after consideration of the rock and debris strewn floor of the forest, he squashed the idea.

After another agonizing thirty minutes, he yelled curses at the top of his lungs. Not only was he finding no indication she had taken the path he was on, but the heat and exertion coupled with the agony in his feet made him miserable. Ivan decided he needed to stop and think. Furthermore, he had no clue where he was as his phone GPS was not picking up a signal. He took some consolation in thinking she didn't know where she was either. Surely, she was as tired and thirsty as he was and would have stopped to rest as well. If he were to make a lateral search in both directions, he should again be able to pick up the trail. With that resolved, he stood and began searching the wooded area to the right of the trail he was on. It was not long before he spotted a series of broken twigs and depressions in the undergrowth that looked as though weeds had been bruised by someone walking on them.

CHAPTER 6

Lila's phone buzzed. Glancing at the screen, she recognized Quint's number and immediately answered. "What's up? Have you learned something new? I am getting nowhere yet."

"I wanted to alert you that Gerald has urged the President to address the country and explain what is happening. He hopes that world opinion will serve to back the kidnappers down. Even if they back down, there is no guarantee his daughter will be returned unharmed. I would hate to be in his shoes."

"I can't imagine." Lila asked, "Do you know when it will be televised?"

"Shortly. Turn on your television. Gerald says there's one in the office where you are working. All news channels will carry it live."

"I see it." Lila walked over and turned the television on. It immediately tuned to the NBC channel. The moderator was just warning the viewing audience that a Presidential address was eminent. "Are you on the way back here?"

"Not immediately. I'm in conference with Gerald as we decide how to play it from here. I'll call later and let you know when to expect me."

"Okay. I love you."

"Love you, too." Lila watched as the President and his wife

appeared on the screen. They were sitting on a sofa in the living room of their suite. The First Lady clutched a Kleenex that she used to dab at red, swollen eyes. It was obvious she was struggling to regain her composure for the camera. Both of their faces were grim. On a small table beside the sofa was a photograph of their daughter. The camera panned on the photo, then the First Lady, before settling on the President.

Clearing his throat, President Northrup began, "It is with unfathomable sadness that I greet you this afternoon. If you have been watching the news, you are aware that our daughter has been kidnapped and is being held for ransom by foreign agents. When I took the oath of office, it was with a deep awareness of the awesome responsibilities of the Presidency that I swore to put the good of the country above my own. I did not realize at the time that my family would be so imperiled by the office to which I was elected. Perhaps, I should have been more aware of potential dangers. It is hard to put myself into the mindset of those who would perpetrate such a heinous act against a child…not just our child, but any child…to hold, not only her, but our Nation political hostage.

"From the day I took office, I have put the good of the country above my own. I have pledged never to give in to the demands of terrorists both domestic and foreign. I now know just how difficult that stance is for our family, but as President my duty is to my Country before all. As a father and the husband of a grieving mother, it is the hardest decision I have ever made or ever will. I pray that my wife can live with this as she did not make the pledge that I have made, but now must live with the consequences of that oath." The President paused a moment to collect himself. Clearing his throat and reaching for his wife's hand, he continued, "To those foreign governments, or their agents, responsible for seizing my daughter and using her to elicit demands that I cannot fulfill, I ask you to reconsider your actions which ultimately put your countries in needless peril. Your actions will not go unpunished, and your demands will not be met. The United States is joined by our allies in demanding that you release my daughter unharmed. If she is returned safely to us in the next twenty-four hours, we will discuss a mutually agreeable solution to your grievances. Failure to do so will be seen as a hostile action against this Nation. I do not need to remind you of what that entails.

"To my countrymen, I ask your prayers for my daughter, my wife, and me as we face this difficult time. May God Bless us all and God Bless this country."

Lila sat back in her chair, mouth agape. She could not begin to imagine just how difficult that must have been for Dianna's parents. Were she the girl's mother, she doubted she could have sat there and silently endured the speech the President delivered. Lila's musings were cut short by another phone call from Quint. She immediately responded, "I just watched the President. It was gut wrenching."

"That it was. Listen, babe, Buster and I have a lead. Gerald's men tracked Dianna's phone. The signal is weak and intermittent as though it is in an area with poor cellular coverage, but if the battery doesn't die, we hope to locate her. I don't know when we'll get back. I'm calling to let you know what's up. So, don't worry if you don't hear from me for a few hours."

"Stay safe. There's no telling what may be waiting out there," Lila cautioned needlessly. "I love you."

"I love you, too." Quint paused, "I probably won't come

down to where you are because we are in a rush, but I'm going to stop by and pick up Code. Later, babe."

While Lila turned to the corrupted computer that contained the video forwarded by the kidnappers and began working with it, Quint returned to the White House to collected Code. The dog was smart, intuitive, and a good tracker. Quint felt better when his dog was by his side. Furthermore, after hours of being pent up, Code would be eager to get out. He had called in advance to have an unwashed article of Dianna's clothing in a plastic bag and waiting in his room. While Code was no bloodhound, the girl's scent would be helpful.

Buster was waiting on the drive when Quint exited the White House followed by Code. After opening the rear door to let the dog in, he got into the front passenger seat.

"Do you still have a phone signal?"

"Yeah, but it is getting weaker. I also asked Gerald to send a helicopter to circle the general area. I checked the map, and the signal is coming from Prince William Forest Park. It's a large area with nothing much for miles around but trees and creeks. Furthermore, it's rugged and sparsely populated. The helicopter may not get there until after we do. If they pick up anything from the air, they will call me with the coordinates."

"Damn. It sounds like the ideal place to hold someone captive. Does the chopper have heat seeking radar?"

Buster nodded, "Yes. It's standard for this kind of operation. They also are supposed to have a couple of sharpshooters on board. You armed, Quint?"

"Always," Quint patted his shoulder holster where he carried his Glock. He should be insulted that Buster even felt the need to ask, but that was Buster's way. He was a cautious man and that had kept him alive in some dicey situations. Buster was aware that Quint was equally cautious, but he had still asked. Quint chuckled softly. "Okay, let's roll."

Buster stuck his arm out the window and waved at a waiting Secret Service car. It pulled out ahead of them with lights blinking and the siren wailing. With the Secret Service car in the lead, they raced through the city onto their route west with little time wasted. Quint kept his eye on the blinking satellite image generated by Dianna's phone as they followed the lead car.

"Does the guy in that car know where to go?" Quint asked.

"He is linked into the satellite image, too, so he will get us there as fast as possible. Once they get fueled and in the air, the whirlybird should give us a valuable assist over a large area that would be difficult on foot."

*****

Dianna sat down on the edge of the creek. Pulling the bottle of water from the bag she took a long drink. Holding the bottle up to the light, she could see there was less than half remaining. She would have to be careful to restrict herself to only an occasional sip as she did not know how far she would have to go to reach civilization. She next pulled out the protein bar, broke it in half and ate it. The other half of the bar and the water she returned to her backpack. She was tired and hot. The going was difficult as in places the water was deep forcing her to climb out and edge along the bank. Although she had no way of knowing the name, she was following South Fork Quantico Creek which wandered for miles before finally flowing into Quantico Creek. Mosquitos plagued her, and she was constantly terrified of stepping on a snake. She would love to rest longer, but the sun was already high in the sky. Dianna glanced at her watch. It was already two in the afternoon. She desperately wanted to reach civilization before dark. The idea of spending the night in the forest was terrifying. Despite walking for hours, she had no way of knowing how many more miles awaited. Dianna listened intently but heard no sounds except those of the forest. In a way that was a comfort as it meant no one was immediately on her trail. On the other hand, it meant miles more before she reached a road or house where she could get help.

If she could have known she was no longer being followed, she would not have been as frightened. But she had no way of knowing and could only assume that whoever had taken her would be determined to get her back.

Ivan was limping, scratched from brambles, thirsty and hungry when he finally called it quits. To hell with the bitch, he decided. He hoped she was lying dead in some gully, killed by snakebite or whatever might have befallen a teenager lost in the woods. As he made his way back to the cabin he worried what to do about the missing girl. Without the tapes to provide assurance that she was still alive, their bargaining chip was diminished. When he arrived back at the cabin, he heard the drone of a helicopter in the distance. It appeared to be making a sweeping circle of the area. Worried that the girl had reached help and that they were now on the lookout for him, he began to run ignoring the pain as the heel of his shoes rubbed against blisters that had begun to bleed. When he arrived at the clearing where he had left the car, he snatched open the door. There was no time to search for Barb's phone. He could only hope it was well lost in the woods. In minutes he was flying down the rutted dirt road at a jarring pace.

The first thing he had to do was get with his cohort and plan their next step. It was critical that the President not know that the girl had escaped. If he were to discover that, they would have lost all leverage. The people they worked for did not excuse that kind of mistake. Ivan felt sweat break out on his brow. For the first time in years, he was seriously worried.

Hating the necessity, he picked up his phone and called his partner. "Vassily, we've lost her. The bitch in charge of holding her in the cabin let her get away."

"What?!"

"I had a call from Lena telling me that the President's daughter had managed to break out of the cabin. I told her to wipe it down for fingerprints and any other evidence until I could get there."

"Do you have the video tapes we needed?"

"No, when Lena got there to do the recordings, the girl had already escaped. When I reached the cabin, the two of us searched for her. She got away. I tried my best, but I couldn't find her."

"Proklyatiye! Damn! Get out of there. We have no way of knowing if she has already reached someone and they are searching the area." The leader paused, "Where's Lena?"

Ivan had a momentary vision of the body as it lay in the ravine. "She's taken care of. It will be a long time, if ever, before she's found."

"Good. She always was against my better judgement…too amateurish. I wish I had never let you talk me into using her."

Ivan struggled to control his temper as he cautioned himself to let it pass. It was just like Vassily nailing his mistakes onto someone else. Even so, it rankled him that it was Vassily who had first proposed using Lena. He always seemed to be Vassily's scapegoat and the clean-up detail. At some point, he was going to make him pay for the constant belittlement.

Turning onto the paved highway, he missed hitting the first of two cars coming at a high rate of speed. He thought nothing of it as he sped on his way back to the office he kept in Washington near the Russian Embassy.

CHAPTER 7

Buster swore, "Did you see that asshole? The Secret Service car almost hit him. He pulled out of that dirt road there on the right."

"I did." Quint looked over his shoulder at the speeding car. "And I have a hunch. Turn around and let's go after him. I'll call the lead car to keep following Dianna's phone signal as long as they can. It's so weak I don't think it will last much longer."

While Quint was on the phone with the agency car, Buster sped up to a hundred, slammed brakes and did a perfect Kawalski-moonshiner 180-degree turn.

"Holy crap! Where did you learn that stunt? I thought you were going to kill us both." Quint's knuckles were white from gripping the armrest.

"You liked that, did you?" Buster grinned as he again gunned the engine to over a hundred. "Hang on. I'm going to catch that sorry bastard. Get ready to take his tire out. I'm going to get as close to him as I can so you can get off a shot. Can you do it?"

"Oh, ye of little faith. I'll bet I'm a better shot than you are.

Just drive the damned car and leave the rest to me."

"On it." Buster glanced in the rearview mirror. "The lead car just turned off onto the side road."

Quint turned in the seat and watched as the lead car turned into the road the car ahead of them had just left. "Good. They're turning onto that dirt road you spotted the guy coming from."

Ivan gunned his engine. Looking into his rearview mirror, he saw that one of the cars had turned around and was coming after him. He did not know who it was, but the fact they were now chasing him was not good. He pushed the accelerator to the floor and felt the car surge forward. Whoever was following him was right on his tail. Realizing he was going too fast for the curve just ahead, Ivan braked for all he was worth.

"Bingo. I think you called this one, Quint. Get ready. He's flying, but this car is faster."

Quint lowered his window, flipped the safety off his Glock, and readied for the shot. The moment they were close enough, Quint said, "Hold steady, I'm going for it."

They both watched as the driver's side rear tire blew. The driver of the car struggled to hold it, but at the speed he was going, lost control in the sharp curve. They watched as the car veered off the road and did a slow roll down the embankment.

Ivan did not even hear the bang that caused his car to skew off the road and begin to roll. For the first time since his childhood, he sent a prayer to heaven. It would do him no good. Buster braked their car and brought it to a stop a little beyond the wreck. Backing up, he stopped at the point the other car had left the road. They left their car and were beginning to descend the embankment when a huge explosion followed by a fireball erupted from the crashed vehicle. The heat radiating from the fire forced them to retreat to a safer distance.

Quint shook his head. "We didn't anticipate that. Now, we will never learn what he was up to. We might as well go back to the dirt road and see where it leads. I wonder if the guys in the agency car found anything yet?" Buster said.

"Why don't you give them a call."

"Yeah, might as well. I'm no longer getting a phone signal, so I'm hoping that they got to that phone before the battery went totally dead."

While Quint called, Buster turned the car around. "Hey, this is Quint. Have you all found anything yet?"

"There is an old cabin up ahead. We should be there in a moment. Did you learn anything from that car you were following?"

"No. When we gave chase, the guy gunned it, lost control, and rolled down the embankment. The car exploded before we could get to it and get him out. It's too late to do anything there, except radio in the accident. Maybe forensics can learn something from what's left." In the background, Quint could hear the agency car braking to a stop followed by the slamming of two doors.

"We're at the cabin. There are signs of recent tire tracks here. We are going to recon the area before approaching to make sure we aren't in for a nasty welcome party."

"We'll be there shortly to provide some backup."

"I hear the chopper. So, we should have air support as well."

*****

Dianna had paused to disentangle herself from a briar when she heard a loud boom in the distance. Looking in that direction, she soon saw a column of black smoke rising into the sky. The sound was momentarily alarming, but possibly meant civilization and help. Or did it? With no other option, she decided it offered some hope. Leaving the creek bank, she began to walk in the direction of the smoke. While it lasted, she had a beacon to follow. She was so intent on the column of black smoke that she forgot to pay attention to where she was going. Reaching up to remove a spider-webbed branch from in front of her face, she was unprepared for the next step. With a resounding whump, she landed face first on the needle and leaf-spangled forest floor. Pushing herself up, she struggled to her knees and tried to stand, but her right foot was in a depression. Pulling it out, she rose to her feet and immediately cried out in pain. Sitting back, she rubbed her ankle. It was beginning to swell. She wiggled her toes to make sure nothing was broken before trying to stand again. Putting weight on the bum ankle would make walking an agonizing ordeal. Diana cursed her carelessness. A sprained ankle was going to slow her down. Tears rolled down her cheeks at the thought the smoke would disappear before she found its source. Without it to guide her, she was lost. She no longer heard the creek and thus could not return to it. Refusing to despair, she checked the angle of the sun and determined she was on a southward path. Even if she had to spend the night in the woods, in the morning she only needed to keep the sun on her left shoulder rather than her right. That way, she hoped she could reach the spot where the fire had burned. She refused to consider there might be nothing left there to guide her to civilization. Dianna struggled on.

As the light of the day began to dim, she looked for a spot where she could spend the night in some safety. Only a large tree trunk offered a sort of haven as it seemed to curve into a "C" shape. She sat in the convex curve of the trunk and opened her backpack to retrieve the remainder of her protein bar and the quarter bottle of water that remained. When she had consumed the last of her provisions, she walked a distance away and squatted to relieve herself. She then pulled up her pants and walked back to the tree that was to be her home for the night.

Soon the sky grew dark, and stars twinkled against the velvet blackness. Around her, a chorus of forest creatures began their nocturnal chorus. It had been an eventful day, and she was exhausted. Leaning against the enveloping arms of the tree trunk, she pulled the backpack onto her lap. Despite the pestilent mosquitoes and the throbbing in her ankle, she soon drifted into much needed sleep. Sleeping soundly, she never awakened when a fox crept near enough to sniff at her. Had she been aware, she would have been badly frightened. This was the first time in her life, that she was not only alone in a wilderness…but lost and not knowing if she were still being chased by her abductors.

When the birds twittered in the new day and shafts of sunlight pierced the overhead canopy of leaves, Dianna stirred. Sitting up, she yawned. Reaching into her knapsack, she felt for the bottle of water and a protein bar. She fumbled around inside before remembering she no longer had either. The realization hit her that reaching help was even more imperative if she were to survive. Without water and perspiring from the summer heat, she would soon be desperately thirsty. A growl in her belly reminded her that she had eaten little for over 36 hours. Ruefully she thought about the five pounds she had wanted to lose. Judging by the looseness of her waistband, she figured she had lost even more. She reached up and combed her fingers through her hair, dislodging twigs and leaves as she did so. She chuckled at her predicament as she considered that she at least had found no bugs residing there. Dianna gingerly explored her ankle with her fingertips. It was still sore, but a little less swollen than the day before. Slinging her knapsack over her back, she slowly struggled to her feet trying to keep her weight off her bad ankle until she could test it.

Once she was erect, she put her weight evenly on both feet. The instant twinge of pain assured her that it was going to be a slow slog. Orienting the sun on her left side, she began a limping walk through a forest that seemed endless. After an agonizing hour, Dianna began to look for a broken limb that she could use as a cane to keep her full weight off the injured ankle. In another fifteen minutes, she found one. When she picked it up, it crumbled in her hands from the rot that was consuming it. Tossing it away, she continued a limping walk. It was not long before she found another limb. Testing it, Dianna tried resting some of her weight on it. When it held up, she smiled in triumph.

As the sun rose higher in the sky, it was increasingly difficult to determine the direction. Despite her desperation to get out of the forest, she was concerned that without the sun on her right shoulder she would become more disoriented. She found a clear spot on the forest floor and sat with her head on her knees. The sun beat without mercy on her bowed head. Exposed areas of her skin were beginning to burn. She thought about moving into the shade but was too weary to get up. As the sun slid towards the west, she arose and continued to walk, keeping the sun now on her right shoulder. It was late afternoon when she reached a paved road. Dianna almost laughed with joy; she was so happy to have finally emerged from what had seemed like an endless forest wilderness.

Sinking onto the shoulder of the road, she sat down and waited for a car, a truck, or anything that signaled help to approach her. After an hour of waiting, nothing had arrived. Tired of just sitting, she looked down the road both ways trying to decide which direction to take. Standing up and taking the left, she started walking. She had walked for maybe half an hour when she came to skid marks on the road. Looking over the side, she saw the burned-out area at the bottom of the embankment. She could not help but wonder what had happened, and if someone had been hurt in an accident. *This is the source of the smoke that I saw yesterday,* she thought.

Desperately thirsty and hungry, Dianna wanted to cry with frustration that no traffic seemed to frequent the road, nor she had seen any dwellings that offered the possibility of rescue. Squaring her shoulders, she continued to walk as the sun set behind her. When dusk announced the eminent arrival of night, she sank down on a weedy area just down from the shoulder of the road. Dianna thought about staying on the verge where a passing motorist could spot her, but she was afraid her abductors would be looking for her, thus she walked down the embankment until she was out of sight.

Tired, hungry, thirsty, and throbbing with pain, she had no choice but to rest as her ankle was increasingly painful. Stuffing her knapsack under her head for a pillow, she drifted off into a troubled sleep. She was awakened by the sound of thunder. The wind rose, and lightning crackled across the heavens followed by heavy rain. Opening her mouth and holding out cupped hands, she drank greedily from this unexpected blessing. When the rain ended, the drop in temperature caused her to shiver. Wet and with no other clothing but the now drenched sweater, she curled into a ball to conserve her body heat and fitfully dozed off and on. She did not hear the two cars that drove by as she dreamed of being murdered by her abductors.

CHAPTER 8

Joe Marshburn and Cory Worley introduced themselves to Quint and Buster when they arrived at the cabin. After the men shook hands, Joe informed the new arrivals, "We checked the cabin. It could have held someone in a room that can be locked from the exterior. We are going to dust it for prints but from the looks of things, it's been wiped clean. The cleaning rags and bleach are sitting inside the front room on the floor. It looks like the window in the back room had boards or something nailed to it. Judging by the gouge marks, it appears they were pried up with a sharp instrument. The marks look fresh as the underlying wood is a lighter color."

Quint and Buster followed the two Secret Service men into the cabin and looked around. They found nothing more than what Joe had reported. Disappointed, Quint started to speak when they were interrupted by the crackling of a radio that Cory carried in a shoulder pack. Cory answered, "Yeah, what's up?" Turning to the other three men, he informed them, "It's the helicopter crew. I'll put it on speaker so you can hear."

They listened intently as the pilot informed them, "We picked up faint body heat in a ravine about a mile from the cabin. It looks like the outline of a body lying on its side. There is nowhere to land but we're going to circle low enough to spray colorant on the tree canopy. We will guide you in. When you see us over the cabin, follow the direction we lead. When you get closer, the paint will let you know where to look. Judging by the level of body heat and the position of the body in the ravine, it doesn't look good. We will circle here until you are ready to follow. Just wave for the go-ahead."

Quint looked at Buster and said, "Let's pray to God it's not Dianna. That is the last thing I want to have to tell the President and his wife."

Quint wasted no time in taking charge by asking Cory to stay at the cabin in the event someone showed up. Buster, Joe, and he would follow the helicopter to the possible body. Looking up, Quint waved to the arriving helicopter to start directing their search. Soon all three men were plowing through the woods at as fast a pace as the irregular ground and undergrowth allowed. After forty-five minutes, they picked up the first sign of color in the treetops. Buster pointed in that direction, and they hastened to the spot where the helicopter was hovering. Scrambling down the embankment into the ravine, they began to look around.

Quint was the first to notice something wrong. "Let's look over there. Those leaves are wet on top which means they've been stirred up. We'll do a little digging and see if there is something underneath those leaves that caused the helicopter to pick up a heat signal.

Joe was the first to yell, "There's a body."

"Is it Dianna?" Quint held his breath as he waited for the answer.

"I don't think so. Help me clear away the rest of these leaves and see what you think."

In moments, the body of the girl was uncovered. Her mouth was slack, her eyes open, and her limbs were beginning to stiffen indicating the beginning of rigor mortis. Buster knelt and gently closed her eyes. "This looks like the description of Dianna's friend that went missing the same time she did."

Quint stood up and took out his phone. The CIA director picked up on the first ring. "Gerald, we think we have Dianna's friend. The girl's been shot. Her body is in a ravine about a mile from a cabin in the middle of Prince William State Park. The helicopter crew picked up body heat, so she's been dead no more than a few hours."

"Any sign of Dianna?"

"Not yet. We'll keep looking."

"Let's hope she got away," Gerald said. "I'm sending a forensics team to document the crime scene and remove the body. If you leave the location, station someone at the cabin that can lead them to the body."

"Cory is on cabin detail now. By the way, we need you to send someone to a crash site on the small road about a half mile before the turnoff for the cabin. Have them take the Joplin Road past Joplin. When they come to the fork, there's a sharp right onto a smaller road. The wreck is probably 3-4 miles down on the left side. It's still putting up a good column of smoke. If they get there quick enough, the smoke will tell them where to look. The guy driving the car is pretty much cinders by now, but forensics may be able to pick up something from what's left. To get to the cabin, stay on that small side road until you see a gravel turn off on the right. That will lead them to the cabin. We also need a cast of the tire tread marks on the side of the road and another cast of those at the cabin to see if there's a match."

"Could a chopper land on the road at the crash site or at the cabin?"

"Not a chance. That entire road is not much more than a paved path and there's a thick tree canopy."

"I should have someone there in less than an hour." Gerald paused before continuing, "The body of Dianna's friend is upsetting news, if that is the identity of the body. I'm going to hold off telling the President while you look for Dianna. I'm hoping she escaped, but that is one hell of a big forest. Lots of hills, creeks, and miles of forest. Not to mention snakes and animals that could pose a danger. She could be wandering around lost out there somewhere."

"I agree. There's no point in causing the First Family any more worry until we know something for sure."

"Right. The chopper is continuing to search in an expanding pattern. If Dianna's out there, they should be able to locate her. The only issue that could prolong the search is a severe weather front moving in. If it gets rough, they'll have to land somewhere and ride it out."

"Damn. I hope the agents you are sending will be able to take casts of the tire tracks before it rains."

"They are on the way now. While we were talking, I texted my assistant to take care of it."

"We will hang around until forensics gets here. There is nothing we can do that the chopper with heat seeking radar cannot do better."

"Stay in touch. If I learn anything new, I'll call. Until then, hope the storms go around us."

By the time the forensics team reached the cabin, the clouds were low and dark, and the wind was picking up, rapidly lowering the temperature. They wasted no time getting to the murder scene to get as much done as they could before it began to rain. A large tarpaulin would be draped over the site to protect it if necessary. The men assured Quint that they had the tire cast from the accident scene and would shortly have one from the cabin. At that point, Buster and Quint decided there was little more they could do. Lightning lit up the sky as they drove away. Glancing up, they saw the chopper leaving the area. It would not return until it was safe to resume the search.

Buster shook his head, "Poor girl. If she is out there, she's in for a rough night."

"Yeah. Let's join the chopper patrol tomorrow. I suspect with their technology we will have a better chance of finding her." He left unsaid: *or her body.*

*****

Dianna could not remember ever having been so cold and miserable. The grass prickled her skin, mosquito bites itched, she was thoroughly soaked from the driving rain. Shivering from the cold, she stood up and tried exercising to increase her body heat. With a gimpy ankle it was impossible to do more than swing her arms and hop on her one good leg. After fifteen minutes, she felt a little warmer. Again, she curled up on the wet ground and tried to conserve as much body heat as possible. Fitful sleep claimed her. She awakened as dawn was beginning to cast a golden glow in the sky promising a cooler day free of rain. As the sun climbed, she felt herself beginning to thaw from the chilly night. The rain had diminished her thirst but done nothing for her hunger. Standing and gingerly resting her weight on her injured ankle, she squared her shoulders and prepared to resume walking to what she could only hope would be safety.

As she made her way down the road, she spotted a blackberry bramble loaded with ripe berries on the lowest part of the road bank. The pitch was steep, and she feared trying to descend with her ankle still injured and the stick only of moderate help. The growling of her stomach convinced her she should try to reach the berries. Sitting down, she began to inch her way down the slope. Once she reached the bottom, she stood up and hopped from bush to bush, cramming ripe berries into her mouth. Soon her mouth and hands were stained with the dark juice of the ripe berries. Momentarily satisfied, she sat down and worked her way back up the slope, using her hands and pushing with her good leg to navigate upward to where she had left her stick and knapsack.

Dianna looked inside the sack. There was nothing there that would help her in her current situation. She had the stylus she used to pry the boards and that could serve as a weapon if needed, but the books were only an unnecessary burden that she did not need. If she ever made it back to school, she could purchase more. She decided that they held no importance and only added to her burden in the current situation. Fishing out the stylus, she shoved it into her shorts pocket careful not to push it in so far that it would poke her. She left the knapsack on the ground and began walking in a direction she hoped would lead to safety. Not knowing if a passing car was that of one of her abductors or someone else, she decided to avoid detection by staying on the very edge of the road where she could quickly get out of sight should she hear an approaching auto. If she could reach a gas station or house, she would feel much safer about making her identity known.

By mid-morning she was both hot and thirsty, and hunger again plagued her. Doggedly, she ignored her miseries and trudged ahead, one laborious step after another. She began to doubt herself and to wonder if she had come in the wrong direction, but the idea of turning around and going back the way she had come was too devastating to consider.

As the sun crept higher in the sky, she realized she needed to stop and rest. Clambering back down the slope on the side of the road, she found a spot under the shade of a bush and curled up for a nap. She could not have said how long she had slept, but the shadows had grown longer when she awakened. Her empty stomach and dry mouth reminded her that if she were to survive, she needed to find more berries to sustain her. Staying at the bottom of the slope she hobbled along until she found another blackberry bush. Again, she ate her fill, but the cramping in her stomach reminded her that nothing but a berry diet was not going to be a happy one. After relieving herself, she wished she had torn some pages from the books she had tossed away to use for cleaning herself.

Dianna bit back her tears, as a sudden bout of diarrhea forced her to stop and again relieve herself. She realized that unless she found rescue soon, she would not make it. She was tired, weak, dehydrated, hungry, and her ankle was a continuous throb. The diarrhea was only going to worsen the dehydration. Struggling back up the slope to the road, she continued onward. Surely she would soon see signs of a dwelling or business.

After thirty minutes, she could walk no more. Sinking to the road in despair, she did not at first hear a helicopter circling above the canopy of trees. Surely, the kidnappers were not coming for her with a helicopter. Praying that exposing herself was not a mistake, Dianna crawled into the middle of the road and waited. In minutes, the chopper hovered overhead, and a man leaned out with a bull horn. "Stay there. We are here to help you. We are going to lower a chair to you. When it reaches you, will you be able to strap yourself in? If you can, just wave your right hand. If you don't think you can do it, we will send someone down to help you."

Tears of relief rolled down her face as she shook her head. In short order, a rope dangled from the chopper tied to a chair lift with a man seated in it. She watched anxiously as the man descended. The pilot jockeyed the whirlybird until the chair was mere feet from her. Loosening the strap that held him in the seat, the man rushed to her side, picked her up, and carried her to the chair. Holding her in his lap, he secured a seatbelt around them. Buster instructed from the open chopper door, "Are you secure, Quint? Wave your hand if you are, and we will pull you up."

When they reached the chopper, Buster leaned out and pulled them in. When they were securely inside, Quint loosened the strap on the chair before carrying her to a seat against the wall.

"Are you Dianna Northrup?"

"Yes. Please call my parents and let them know I'm okay. I'm just weak and I hurt my ankle."

"They are going to be beyond happy to hear we found you. My name is Quint Cord; my partner here is Buster Walton. Your father hired us to find you." Quint reached into his pocket and pulled out his cell phone. After pulling up the President's private number, he handed the phone to her and said, "Text your father and let him know you are on the way to Walter Reed Hospital. We are going to have the doctors check you out to make sure you are okay. They'll probably Xray that ankle."

Dianna took the phone and did as instructed. When she had finished, she handed the phone back to Quint and asked, "I am so thirsty. Do you have any water?

Buster leaned over and handed her a bottle of Deer Park. "Want a candy bar?"

"Oh, my gosh, I would love it. I am about starved to death." Quint glanced over at her and wondered how to tactfully inquire if she had been abused. After a moment, he said, "Dianna, were you harmed or abused in any way while you were held in captivity."

She shook her head, blushing as she caught his meaning. "No. The only person I saw was the girl I thought was my friend. Instead, she was in on my kidnapping. I don't know what happened to her, but I don't think it was good as I heard a gunshot from the direction of the cabin while I was running. I hate to think that those she was working with would kill her because I escaped."

"Don't feel guilty about. It isn't your fault. She chose to cooperate with some very evil characters. That never turns out well."

Dianna looked over at Quint, "Did they kill her?"

Quint bit his lower lip before replying, "We think so. We won't know for sure until forensics are finished with the body we found."

Dianna nodded without speaking. A single tear rolled down her cheek before she drew in a deep breath and turned her head away. Now she would never know why Barb had done what she did.

CHAPTER 9

President Northrup and his wife arrived at Walter Reed hospital shortly after Dianna was settled in a room. Already the CIA, working with hospital security, had tightened up surveillance of the hospital. The wing where she was being treated for dehydration was entirely sealed off from the rest of the hospital. Security agents were posted at every entry, stairwell, and elevator. All access points required photo ID and a reason for admission. Not even doctors and nurses were exempted. Gerald Williams was taking no chances that the President's daughter would again be abducted.

Tightly holding his wife's hand, President Northrup walked up to Quint Cord and Buster who were manning security at the door to Dianna's room. He shook both men's hands and gave them his heartfelt gratitude. Mrs. Northrup ignored their outstretched hands and gave both Quint and Buster a hug. Her eyes were shining with tears.

"We can't begin to thank you enough for all you have done to recover our daughter. Both the President and I are forever in your debt."

"Mrs. Northrup, I have experienced the pain that you and your husband have suffered. The day my wife was abducted was the worst time of my life. I was so happy when we were able to rescue Lila and she had not been harmed. I'm thrilled both she and your daughter survived their ordeals with little consequence," Quint replied.

President Northrup said, "We cannot begin to repay the debt we owe you for recovering Dianna. If you men ever need anything, let me know. If it's in my power, you'll have it."

"Thank you, sir." Both Quint and Buster responded.

"We'll go in now and see Dianna. Do you know if the doctor has been by?"

"He's with her now."

"Good. I want to hear how she's doing."

"We understand." Buster smiled, "Dianna's been asking for you…along with ice cream, a hamburger and fries, and a big soft drink. By the way, it's ordered and already on the way."

Mrs. Northrup laughed, "That sounds like my girl."

The President and Mrs. Northup entered the room to find the doctor checking Dianna's chart. He looked up and smiled, "Mr. President, you have a tough little lady here. We'll keep her another day just to be sure, but she's doing fine. We are giving Dianna an IV to rehydrate her and a bland diet for today. There's nothing broken in the ankle, just a bad sprain. It's bandaged and we are keeping it elevated. If all goes well, you can take her home tomorrow."

The First Lady wiped the tears that welled in her eyes before she walked over. Her lower lip was trembling as she held her daughter's hand after first giving her a hug and a kiss on the forehead.

The President smiled at Dianna before turning to the doctor and saying, "I gather my daughter has already ordered her evening meal: hamburger and fries…not exactly a bland diet. Is that going to be a problem?" The doctor paused and turned back.

He chuckled before responding, "It would probably be worse for her morale if I said no. If she thinks she can handle it, we will let it be her call."

Bidding the doctor goodbye, the President stood for a moment to get his emotions under control before he joined his wife on the opposite side of the bed to hold his daughter's other hand.

"I'm so sorry, Mom and Dad. I have put you through a lot that wouldn't have happened if I had just listened to you. Please, forgive me. I've learned a hard lesson." Tears sprang to her eyes as she added, "I don't tell you often enough, but I love you so much. You're the best parents."

Her father smiled, "Don't blame yourself, darling. The people that did this are the guilty ones. We will pray this never happens again. The thing now is to be thankful that we have you back and unharmed. We intend to keep it that way. If you need anything, let the nurses know. Your Secret Service agent is stationed outside your door. He's going to stick to you like Velcro from now on."

"It's not Mr. Atkins' fault I got taken. Please tell him I am so sorry. I avoided him and trusted someone I thought was a friend."

"We all need friends. And all of us have been let down by one at some time or another. We know adjusting to all of this has been hard for you."

Quint walked in followed by Buster bearing Dianna's requested dinner. "I think this is for you, Miss Northrup."

Dianna beamed at the sight of the food. "Wonderful. I am going to enjoy every bite!"

Mrs. Northrup leaned over and kissed Dianna's forehead,

"Get some rest, darling. We will be back to get you in the morning. We love you to the moon and back. I thank God you are back and unharmed."

The President shook Quint and Buster's hands. "I will leave my daughter in your care."

Quint said, "Don't worry, sir. We are going to do our best to keep her safe."

The President and his wife closed the door softly on the way out. Buster had just wheeled Dianna's tray to the bedside and placed her food on it when a loud bang rang out shaking the room and its inhabitants. Both Quint and Buster were knocked to the floor. Momentarily stunned, they slowly gained their feet and stood. Their ears were ringing with sounds coming to them like they were underwater. Shaking his head to clear it, Quint looked at Dianna who appeared to be in shock. He asked, "Are you okay?"

She shook her head as though to clear her own ears before replying, "I'm okay. What happened?"

"We don't know. You go ahead and have your dinner. We will check things out," Buster said as he caught Quint's eye.

"Right. Dianna we're going to see what happened. You are going to be fine so try not to worry. We'll be back to let you know as soon as we know what's going on."

Both men drew their weapons prior to opening the door to peer into the hall. Quint stepped out first with Buster hard on his heels. The scene before them was a disaster zone. There were bodies on the floor that were covered with fragments of ceiling tile. Only dim light from a window at the end of the hall illuminated the scene, but that was enough to show the damage. Slowly some of the bodies began to stir. The first to sit up and brush off the debris that covered him was Dianna's guard, Agent Atkins. Putting his gun in his waist band, Quint stepped over a ceiling tile and helped him to his feet while Buster began to check the others. Atkins looked around him in dismay. Clearly in shock, he began to tremble as he pointed at the bodies. "The President..."

"Oh, my God!" Quint exclaimed as he joined Buster in clearing debris from the inert bodies on the floor. Each man bent to feel for a pulse before shaking his head and moving on to the next. Several of the agents on duty in the hallway prior to the explosion began to move. One or two, groaning in agony, had been pierced by the metal grid holding up the ceiling tiles. Two others were obviously dead. Quint was the first to spot the President and first lady near the open elevator door. Neither of them was moving. Hurrying over, he called Buster to come help. Feeling for the President's pulse, he was thrilled to feel a faint thread. He next turned to the First Lady. Getting no pulse, he began to do CPR. Buster scrambled over the debris and began to check the unconscious President for injuries.

After a couple of minutes, the President seemed to be coming to. Buster put a restraining hand on his shoulder. "Try to stay still. We are going to get you and the others some help."

"My daughter?" Northrup asked as he opened his eyes. "She's fine and in her room having her dinner. Don't worry about her."

"My wife?"

"Quint's helping her now. Just stay calm. Atkins just called for medical assistance, so doctors are on the way." Buster glanced over at Quint who paused long enough to shake his head before returning to his efforts to save Mrs. Northrup.

"What happened?" the President asked.

"There was an explosion. We don't know who, how, or why. I am going to call Director Williams and let him know what is going on. You just keep still until the doctors arrive. You've got some nasty gashes that I need to stop bleeding."

As Buster tied a tourniquet around the President's leg using his tie, Northrup said, "I understand." Glancing over to his wife's prone body on the floor, he struggled to sit up. "Is she hurt? She's not moving. Is she dead? Oh, my God, not my Mary!"

Buster pressed him back to the floor, "Quint's helping her. The best thing you can do is keep calm, Mr. President. We are doing our best to help everyone here. If your wife were dead, Quint would not still be with her." Buster doubted that was true. In the distance they could hear the blare of sirens as police from all over the area rushed to the scene. Coming up the stairwell, as the elevators on that wing were still inoperative, was a battalion of doctors and nurses followed by three more of Gerald Williams' security detail. They all looked shell-shocked. Quint supposed he and Buster did not look much better. He moved away from Mary Northrup as a doctor began to check her vitals. He had known for some minutes it was no use. She had died almost immediately from the blast.

Buster was standing near the President watching the doctor who was working to control the bleeding. As they placed the President on a gurney and wheeled him down the hall, Buster glanced over at Quint and motioned to the far end of the hall. As they left the immediate scene, more gurneys arrived to remove the wounded for treatment and to take the dead to the morgue.

Both men quietly walked away and turned to stare back at the hall. Buster nodded his head towards the bomb scene, "So, what is the first thing that comes to mind?"

"I suspect we are both thinking the same thing. Someone in the security detail is a traitor, and either set the bomb, or enabled someone else to."

"This looks too professional for amateurs. The question is whether or not that 'someone else' is the same bunch that snatched Dianna."

"I suspect that's true. The minute the news media blasted it out that she was rescued, her kidnappers had a good idea we would take her to the government's secure hospital. We also need to ferret out how our security was penetrated in record time to set the bomb, or if the plant was already in place."

Buster glowered, "If I find the guy, somebody had better stop me or I will kill his ass before they can arrest him. He killed the First Lady for Christ's sake. That woman never harmed a fly."

"When you consider the speed with which the bomb was planted in the specific wing housing Dianna, you can't help but think they had already infiltrated someone into the security detail, or they turned someone that was already there. We need to find out whether there were any recent hires and if any of the existing personnel was in financial difficulty...or had politics that suggest animosity to the President that goes beyond the normal opposition. And we have to figure out how this ties into whoever kidnapped Dianna."

"Quint, Buster!"

They turned to see the CIA Director, Gerald Williams hurrying their way. "Damnation!" he erupted as he halted mere feet from them. "What in the hell happened? This place was supposed to be locked down tight."

Quint glanced at Buster before replying, "We were just

talking about that. Judging by how quickly this was set up, we think we may have a plant in the security detail either from the CIA, the Secret Service, or the Walter Reed security."

Gerald looked thunderous. He growled, "Who was hurt?"

"The First Lady was killed along with two agents from the President's detail. Two others are badly hurt. The President was bleeding heavily from a wound to his leg. The President and the other injured are all on their way to the operating room. The bodies were taken to the morgue, I assume. The other agents in the hall were shaken up but nothing serious. Atkins is back guarding the door to Dianna's room. He suffered a few scratches, but he's fine."

Nodding towards the door where Atkins was standing guard, Gerald asked, "And the President's daughter?"

"Dehydrated, a sprained ankle, but nothing serious. She wasn't injured by the blast and since we were in her room, we weren't either. In fact, she's having her dinner. She doesn't yet know about her mother."

Gerald surveyed the scene. His mouth went down at the corners, and he shook his head as he studied the damage. "Apparently the bomb was not meant for her, but for the President when he visited her. Whoever set the bomb off had to know he was in the hallway at that precise moment before the elevator arrived. The question is what and who triggered the bomb before the door opened and the President and his wife could get on."

Buster looked at Quint, who nodded for him to go ahead. "I suspect the culprit could have been watching the elevator arrive from another floor and triggered it remotely as the elevator arrived."

Quint agreed, "That is a possibility and would keep whoever it was out of the danger zone. The other options are that it was one of the injured agents, or one of the two that were killed."

Gerald pointed to the camera that monitored the hallway. "It could have been done by someone monitoring the camera either here at Walter Reed, or if they hacked in, from a remote location. That still leaves the question of the speed with which the bomb was planted. I agree that suggests an inside job."

Quint nodded, "It could be that the bomber has been here a while and laying low until he was called on by whoever turned him. Either that, or the background investigation before he was hired was deficient."

Gerald nodded, "Good questions. Believe you me, my men are going to comb through every man's file we have on these security details. I also am going to find out who besides security serviced this wing. We will be running a background check on every one of the staff to see if there is something in their immediate circumstances that would have led them to cooperate with whoever is behind this and the kidnapping. That means we check doctors, nurses, aides, cleaning staff, etc. We will find the culprit. That is a promise."

CHAPTER 10

The sea of black umbrellas was scant protection from the pouring rain that drenched those forced to stand around the tent where the graveside service was being conducted. From where Quint and Lila stood under their own giant umbrella, Quint could see the faces of both the President and his daughter as they stood by the First Lady's grave. Both faces were wet with tears.

On the edge of the cemetery, smiling with grim satisfaction, Vassily and his boss watched as the mourners arrived. They could not help chuckling when they considered the next surprise. Quint had talked with the President and Dianna the previous evening following the wake. They were both suffering not only from Mary Northrup's death, but from a deep sense of guilt. No matter what Quint said to reassure them they were not to blame, both felt they were justified in their feelings. The President said that had it not been for him winning the Presidency, his daughter would never have been abducted, and possibly murdered, and his wife would still be living.

For Dianna having befriended the wrong person that would result in her own kidnapping, she felt that her mother's death would never have happened except for that tragic mistake. The fact that her father had almost suffered the same fate as her mother only exacerbated her feelings of deep remorse. The

President and Dianna had sat side-by-side on the sofa in their living room on the second floor of the White House. Quint and Lila sat across from them as they tried to offer support and encouragement. Especially troubling to Quint and his wife was the President's threat to resign from the Presidency and take his daughter far from Washington and the dangers associated with the office.

Standing up and walking over to the President, Lila leaned over and squeezed his hand. In a soft voice, she said, "Mr. President, Mary would not want you to give up. She believed in you and what you represent to this country. You need to stay here and fight to bring the people who did this to justice. Justice for not only your wife, you and your daughter, but for this nation. We are all grieving with you and support you in this horrible time. This country is not only with you, but it's angry that such a thing could happen to our First Lady. This country will never be safe from these murderers and others like them if we do not stand strong and determined. We need you. Your pain is personal, but your sworn duty to this country is to assure this doesn't happen again."

Clay Northrup squeezed her hand and without looking up, he cleared his throat and replied, "Thank you. Of course, you are right. It's a hard thing to face as I want to take Dianna, leave this town, and never look back, but I know that is not what Mary would want."

Dianna wiped angry tears from her eyes, before declaring, "Daddy, we're going to make sure these people pay. I don't want you to give up now. We're going to fight them and we're going to win. You are not to blame for any of this. It was my own stupidity."

"Darling, you are not to blame any more than your father. We all need friends, and no one blames you for thinking Barb meant you well. You were a victim of evil people just as your mother was…and sadly, so was your friend Barbara," Lila reassured her. As Quint recalled the conversation in his mind, he watched as military personnel in vans stationed themselves on the driveway. Despite the size, the entire perimeter of the cemetery at Arlington was surrounded by security guards standing six feet apart. The cemetery, which was tightly controlled, had been swept clean two days previous and no one had been allowed in until the time for the burial. Gerald Williams had shut down the airspace over Arlington for twenty miles around. The only things he could not stop flying were birds and insects. No one without an invitation had been allowed through the sole checkpoint. No one was taking any chances that there would be another attempt on the President's life during the televised ceremony. Even that was restricted to the local NBC network that had undergone extensive vetting and was attended by National Guard troops on high alert.

Director Williams was standing a short distance to the right of Quint and Lila. Quint watched Buster constantly scan the grounds of the cemetery, phone in hand. He knew his friend was appalled that the security to protect the First Family had been breached. Gerald Williams, too, felt guilty that the CIA and various other security services had not been sufficiently thorough in their protocols.

Quint watched as Buster walked over to join Gerald. After a discussion, he could not hear, Buster began walking toward the television crew. After a few minutes' of talking with one of the people in the crew, Buster nodded his head and walked back to the Director. Although Quint could not tell what was said, he assumed it was either a false alarm or nothing of real importance. Neither man saw Vassily and his partner leave.

Suddenly the hairs on the back of his neck stood up. Puzzled by the unease, Quint shifted his umbrella and scanned the area, but he could see nothing to cause alarm. Detecting a buzzing noise that sounded like dozens of angry bees, he squinted at the sky. It took him a moment to realize that the pings he heard were not hail, but bullets of some type coming from what appeared to be drones circling in the leaden skies.

Grabbing Lila's hand, he sprinted towards the President and his daughter. Without hesitation he pushed the President, Dianna, and Lila into the hole under the catafalque where they were protected by the burial vault. He then tucked himself above them for further protection of both them and his own life. Around him he heard the screams of the wounded and the shouts of others rushing to safety. Beyond the shredded tent, bodies carpeted the area between the gravestones. He found it difficult to believe that anyone could survive the hail of bullets that came from every direction. He could not see Buster or Gerald Williams. He could only pray that they were safe as his friendship with them both was rare and among the most important ones in his life.

After what seemed like hours but had been no more than a couple of minutes, the attack from the drones stopped and Quint could hear them as the buzzing they made became ever fainter. Moving out from under the vault, he leaned down. With the President's help he first pulled Lila up and then Dianna, warning them to stay low in case the drones returned. He then reached down and helped Northrup climb out of the excavation for his wife's grave. Water dripping from the dozens of holes ripped in the tent above their heads sounded like heavy tears as they fell on the casket holding the First Lady.

"Thank you, Quint." The President made a grim chuckle. "It would appear it is unsafe to be anywhere near me since I refused to negotiate the kidnappers' demands."

"They are definitely playing hardball." Quint motioned to the surrounding area where some of those that had huddled behind graves and under cement benches were beginning to stand. "I'll leave our ladies with you while I see what I can do to help the ones that were hurt. I can hear sirens, so I suspect police and ambulances are on the way. Stay here and duck back down if you hear anymore drones."

"Go. Do what you can. We're going to be fine."

Giving Lila a quick hug, he said, "Stay with the President, Lila. I love you and will be back as soon as I can assess what is happening."

Lila squeezed his hand, "I love you, too."

Quint hurried away from the three of them as his eyes constantly scanned the scene for any danger from another quarter. Orienting himself to where he last saw Gerald and Buster, he hastened in that direction. As he approached, he saw numerous bodies on the ground...some groaning and moving weakly and others beginning to stir. Recognizing the clothes Buster had worn to the ceremony, he hurried over as Buster began to sit up.

Kneeling beside him, he put his hand on his friend's shoulder, "Buster, don't move until I can check you for injuries."

Buster shook his head, "Don't worry about me. It's just a flesh wound. I can handle it. I tell you I just knew something was off. I could feel it, but I had nothing but intuition to go on. I walked over to the television crew to see if that was causing the angst, but they all checked out. I'm sorry I couldn't stop it."

"Hey, man. It's not your fault. You did what you could."

"Yeah, and it amounted to nothing." Buster shook his head with disgust before pointing to his left. "Gerald is over there behind the headstone…the one that says Henderson…I think he may be badly hurt."

Quint paused anyway and checked Buster's side to ascertain that the wound was not life threatening before hurrying in the direction Buster indicated. On the ground behind the large funerary monument, Gerald lay motionless. Blood was pulsing steadily from a wound in his arm. Quint whipped a knife from his pocket and ripped Gerald's sleeve from the wound. Judging from the blood, he suspected an artery had been nicked but not totally ruptured. He wasted no time in removing his necktie and using it as a tourniquet around Gerald's left arm. Once the bleeding slowed, he began checking for other injuries. The bullet had gone through the arm leaving an exit wound which meant doctors wouldn't have to go in to extract a bullet. A large lump on his forehead indicated that Gerald must have fallen and hit his head on the monument when he was shot.

As Quint checked his friend's pulse, Gerald opened his eyes and blinked. "Damnation, Quint. What in the hell just happened here?"

"That is the 'sixty-four thousand-dollar' question. The President and his daughter are both safe. I am going to get them into the Presidential limo and back to the White House. Help is coming and will get you to the hospital shortly. Your injury does not appear to be life threatening, but this bleeding must be stopped. You also need to be checked for a possible concussion as you have one humongous lump on your head."

Gerald attempted to grin. It was a weak effort as he grimaced with pain. "Thanks, Quint. Don't worry about me. Just get the President to safety."

"Do you think we should take him to the bunker until we know what's going on?"

"Absolutely. He's not going to like it, but we can't take any chances."

Quint patted Gerald's shoulder, "Good luck."

"Thanks, you, too."

As Quint walked away, he heard Gerald on his phone giving orders to his agents. Someone would have to answer for the invasion of the enemy drones and why they were not detected before they could attack. When he arrived at the catafalque, he saw that the President cuddled his daughter in his arms. Lila, who was sitting to one side, immediately stood when he reached her.

"What now, Quint?"

Instead of a direct answer to her, he turned to the President, "Mr. President, you, Dianna, and Lila are coming with me. We need to run as fast as we can for your limo. It's the safest place you can be. When we get there, I'm going to take down the flags on the car. If the driver is unhurt, he's going to take us to the White House. If he cannot, I will drive. We need to get out of here fast in case there is another attack. Someone triggered this. They could still be here and know that you survived."

The President glanced at his daughter and Lila, "Come on ladies, let's pretend we're running a race and the goal is that big black car over there. Now, go."

The three of them raced for the limo with Quint bringing up

the rear. When they reached the car, The President, Lila, and Dianna immediately got in and closed the door. Quint breathed a sigh of relief knowing they were safe. Next, he looked around for the chauffeur and the secret service detail that had remained with the car. Judging by the motionless bodies around the car, driving back to the White House would be up to him.

Walking to the front of the car, he hastily ripped off the flags. He then checked the ground for a clear path to the exit that would not run over any of the dead or injured. As several were in the way, he walked over and tugged them to the side of the route he would take. Checking to ensure that he had a clear path, Quint hurried back to the limo and climbed behind the wheel. He lowered the window between the driver's compartment and the passenger area.

"Mr. President, I am going to take a different route back to the White House than the way we came. It's a little longer but I hope it will be safer."

"Do what you need to do. You're in charge of this."

"Thank you, sir."

Quint started the limo and headed in the direction of McClellan Gate where he turned left. He then turned onto the street that would take them over the bridge on the Potomac River to the traffic circle around the Lincoln Memorial. From there he drove to 17Th Street where he turned right at Lafayette Square. Immediately he turned in the drive to the White House. It was obvious they were expected as agents in the ubiquitous black suits and ear devices lined the portico entrance to the White House.

The President leaned toward the partition window, "Thank you for getting us back, Quint. We should be fine now."

"I'm sorry, sir. We cannot trust that. My orders are to get you into the bunker until we are certain you're safe."

"I'm fine, but it's imperative that I speak to the country. People need to know what has happened, that I am unharmed, and we have things under control."

"The bunker is equipped with everything you need to make a televised address and to keep you safe. In this, you are overruled, Mr. President."

Dianna took her father's hand, "You need to trust Quint to keep us safe. If he thinks this best, we need to do it."

Northrup muttered under his breath as he followed Dianna into the house. Holding his hand, Lila walked with Quint. Softly she asked, "Will we need to stay in the bunker long?"

"I wish I knew, darling. I just wish I knew. But, until we do, you are going to be in the safest place in Washington."

Lila snorted, "You mean I'm going to be in the center of the bull's eye."

Quint shook his head but did not answer. "Well?" she challenged.

"Babe, I don't know what's going on. But that bunker with all the security built into it and with all the agents on the grounds and in the house determined to ensure the President's safety, you should be fine."

"I should be fine?? What about you? Are you going to be in the bunker with me?" Lila struggled to swallow back a gathering hysteria.

"If I'm more useful on the outside trying to get to the bottom of all of this, I will have to leave. For the moment, though, I'll stay with you all. Gerald will be on to this the minute they are through treating him. I suspect Buster and Gerald's men are already digging for the source of those drones."

"Is Gerald okay?"

"He was hurt, but he's going to be fine."

Quint took her elbow as they followed the President and Dianna, who in turn were following a secret service agent, into the bowels of the White House. At their backs were a dozen additional agents. He suspected some would be stationed in the bunker as a last-minute defense while others would be posted at the sealed entrance.

When they reached the heavily reinforced door, Quint watched as Northrup squared his shoulders and took a deep breath. He recalled hearing that as a child, Northrup had accidently locked himself in an abandoned refrigerator and nearly died before he was rescued. Since that time, the man had a horror of sealed spaces. This would be a nightmare for him.

CHAPTER 11

Quint and Buster were sitting by Gerald Williams bedside at Walter Reed as they watched the latest newsfeed on CBS which followed on the heels of the President's address to the nation.

The head anchor, Larry Rivers, shuffled the papers on the desk before him and stared into the monitor. His face then appeared on one side of a split-screen. On the other side of the screen, images of the attack began to scroll. His voice somber, Rivers began:

"Fellow Americans, we are united in both grief and horror at this latest atrocity committed against our President, and those who were in attendance, at our First Lady's graveside service. While we rejoice that the President and his daughter escaped unscathed thanks to the heroic action of Special Agent, Quint Cord, many were not so fortunate. The latest count is 17 dead, 45 injured, and of that number at least 6 are in the hospital fighting for their lives. To the families of those who were so cruelly murdered, we offer our deepest sympathy. For the ones who were injured, the nation joins me in praying for your recovery.

"As the President explained, we do not yet know who is behind this latest attack on the President. Our country's entire investigative services are united in finding the responsible parties and bringing them to justice. President Northrup made clear that he considers these ongoing attacks an act of war against this country. "The Director of the

CIA, Gerald Williams, was also injured in this attack. His office issued a statement saying that Director Williams' injuries are not serious, and he has continued to direct the search for the guilty parties as he undergoes treatment. Secret Service, The Department of National Security, and the FBI are coordinating with the CIA in the investigation.

"If you have information related to the drone attack, please call the number scrolling on the screen. It would be especially helpful if we knew the point of launch for these drones. Contact us if you have seen something suspicious, or you have talked to someone that you feel might have been involved. You do not need to give your name; however, if you identify yourself, there is a reward of one million dollars for information that leads to apprehension of the responsible parties. If you feel more comfortable, go to the front gate at the White House and ask for the Secret Service. You will be taken to a safe place and questioned. If necessary, you will be provided with witness protection.

"As we receive further information, we will continue to keep you informed."

Gerald muted the television before turning to his visitors. "Quint, I want you and Buster to go back and canvas the area in and around the cemetery for a fallen drone. I was able to fire off a couple of rounds before they hit me, so it's possible I brought one of them down."

Quint glanced over at Buster, before nodding his head. "No problem. We are happier doing something constructive than being redundant babysitters at the White House."

Gerald laughed. "Be sure you don't say that to your wife or the President."

Quint chuckled before replying. "I'm not that stupid."

Gerald continued, "Getting back to the drones, we know the

general direction they were coming from and my agents on the perimeter assure me it was not from the cemetery itself. These things came in at a low enough trajectory, they were not picked up by our radar. If we could find one of the drones we would know their manufacturer and be able to compute the range. If we assume they were going to return to their home base, then we cut the range in just over half. That might allow us to determine the point of launch."

Buster and Quint wasted no time saying their goodbyes, both men welcoming their mission. Gerald lay back in his hospital bed totally frustrated that he was not out there in the field with them tracking down clues. That was the major drawback to being promoted to director: other men did the part he most enjoyed while he rode a desk. He closed his eyes, grimacing when he shifted in the bed and an electric shock of pain shot up his arm. He had deployed all his assets; now all he could do was wait and get well enough to leave the hospital. He wanted to be back in the center of operation where information could be more quickly disseminated to critical investigative sources allowing for easier coordination of efforts.

The drive from Walter Reed to Arlington National Cemetery seemed to take forever. Buster swore steadily as they sat in stalled traffic for twenty minutes. Finally, the accident that had created the snarl on the George Washington Memorial Parkway was cleared, and they began to move again. Exiting into the cemetery, Buster drove in the direction of President Taft's grave site near where the first lady had been laid to rest a hundred yards to the right. He stopped the car and he and Quint got out and surveyed the area.

"It's a damned big place for the two of us to cover. I guess the best thing is to start at the First Lady's grave and then work out in circles. Does that work for you, Buster?"

"If we find that drone it is going to be in the firing distance of Gerald's Glock. Optimum accuracy would be less than fifty to seventy-five yards. Drones are relatively small targets so that would reduce the accuracy range. If he got lucky and brought one down, I suspect it is close to where he took cover. I say we start from the Henderson grave where you found Gerald."

"That's an even better idea," Quint agreed. "Let's walk parallel... you go on one side of the graves, and me on the other so we don't miss it. We will do it row by row and check everything within a seventy-five-yard radius."

"Might as well get on it. It's going to take a while."

Four hours later, both men were tired, thirsty, and increasingly frustrated. Sitting on the top of a tombstone, Buster looked over at Quint and said, "This is like looking for a needle in a haystack. It's especially frustrating when we don't even know if he hit one of the damned drones."

"True, but we only have one more row to check. If we find nothing, I say we start checking the perimeter to see if we might learn something. There are a few homeless people that hang out around the bridge. One of them may have seen something."

"You're right. We do one more row and then get the car and start checking along the near shore of the Potomac."

Buster stood up and they began once more to search the area around the tombs. Almost at the end of their search, Quint exclaimed, "This is it. We've found it. It's pretty much intact. It looks like Gerald's bullet took out the main circuit board."

"That was one damned lucky shot."

Quint held up the damaged drone. "Hey, you can read the

manufacturer. Let's Google it and see what kind of range is on the thing."

"What does it say?"

Quint held up the damaged drone, "It's manufactured by Turkish company, ASIS Electronics. This is a Songar Silali System drone. Look at the machine gun mounted underneath. This thing is designed to hold up to 200 NATO class 5.56 X 45- millimeter rounds. The Turks used it in Syria. This thing is not more than three feet wide. Our own government, among numerous other countries, bought some of a larger version of these things from the Chinese…the Wing Loong II drones, and at one to two million dollars each they are not cheap. This little Turkish number is a hell of a lot smaller."

"Yeah, I've read about these Turkish killer drones. If you want to be accurate, the range would be less than 100 meters, but it seemed to me it was just a random spraying of a huge number of bullets based on the theory that that volume of bullets was bound to cause major carnage. The range of this thing means it could have been launched from several miles away." Buster remarked.

"I suspect this one was launched much closer by. That many drones in the air would have been spotted otherwise." Quint picked up the drone, "We'll turn it over to Langley and see what else they can come up with. In the meantime, let's try along the river and see if we can find someone that might have seen where these things were launched."

Walking back to the car, Quint studied the drone. Despite a three-foot wingspan, it was light as only one or two of the large caliber bullets remained in the chambers. "We will have the ballistics team run an analysis on the bullets as well as the rest of this bird. Who knows what we might learn?"

Buster guided the car away from the cemetery and along the drive running along the river. When they neared the bridge over the Potomac, Buster pulled over and parked on the verge. Both men left the car and began walking towards some makeshift camps under the bridge. The smell of unwashed bodies, urine, and feces caused them to catch their breath, but they forced themselves to move closer. Several people were lying on crude pallets, appearing to be either drunk or asleep. Walking on, Quint spotted an elderly man sitting on the bank and staring morosely into water muddied by the recent rain. The man glanced up as they neared and resumed staring at the water. Another man sat several yards away watching their approach with interest.

Quint pointed to the first man, and said to Buster, "You take this one and I'll take that fellow over there."

Quint left Buster to introduce himself and ask the man if he had seen anything out of the ordinary that had occurred the previous day. Walking up to the second man, he did not have a chance to say anything before the man stood up. Although at least seventy, the man looked spry. Intelligence lurked behind his hooded eyes. He was dressed in little better than rags, but he seemed to have made an attempt at grooming, as his hair was neatly combed and his clothes looked and smelled cleaner than those of the other men Quint had passed.

"I been expecting you."

Quint smiled in greeting, "How is that?"

"With all them drones flying over yonder in the cemetery yesterday, somebody was bound to come asking iffn I saw something."

"You're a pretty sharp fellow." Quint chuckled. "If anyone saw anything, something tells me you're the one to ask."

The man nodded his head, "Yeah. I suspect I am. So, what do you want to know?"

"I'm Quint Cord. My partner over there and I were sent here to see if someone might have seen the direction those drones were launched from, or anything else you might have noticed out of the ordinary. You may not know, but a bunch of people were killed and injured in an attack on people attending our First Lady's funeral."

"I figured it was someone important, but since I got no television and don't read the newspapers, I didn't know who it was they was after." The man shook his head and looked down for a moment, before explaining, "My name is Sammy Crenshaw. I fought for this country in Nam. Got a head wound for my trouble, but the worse thing is the memories. I got this thing they call PTSD. I ain't held down a steady job in decades because it hits me sometime, and I guess I kinda go nuts. About three years ago, I moved into the cemetery."

Sammy laughed and pointed towards Arlington Cemetery before continuing, "I figured I was going to end up over there sooner or later anyway. I found a spot inside this house…really a little mausoleum. The plaque on the wall told the name of the fellow it was for and there was a photo of him on a little table. I introduced myself and we became friends like, you know. I would tell him my troubles. Of course, he couldn't really talk back, but I sorta felt like he understood. Besides, in the three years I've live there, he ain't had no company except me. I like it real well and plan on moving back, soon as you government types clear out. I wouldn't have left in the first place except these fellers came and told me I had to clear out of the cemetery for this important funeral. So, I took myself off and moved over here."

Sammy looked down and went silent for several minutes. Quint cleared his throat and said, "I'm sorry you had to move. Now, back to my question: do you recall seeing or noticing anything out of the ordinary that day? Did you notice which direction the drones came in from?"

"Notice?" Sammy laughed and shook his head. "How could I have missed it? They were coming off a barge-like boat anchored right over there that moved in about thirty minutes before all hell broke loose."

"Did you get the name of the boat or the numbers on the hull?"

"Nope. It looked like it had been painted over."

"Sammy, did you notice anyone on the barge or on the shore that might have been guiding those drones?"

"Yeah. There were two of them... one on the barge and one back there in the trees. I thought maybe they were part of the government bunch that was securing everything. Once I heard all them bullets and sirens right after, I knew something won't right."

"What happened after the bullets stopped?"

"Them drones came flying back to the barge then the man in the woods leaped aboard. I heard an engine start, and they hauled ass out of here."

"Going down river or up? Did you get a count of the number of drones."

"Down river. I didn't count them, but there was more than a dozen for sure." Sammy scratched his bewhiskered chin. "Who you reckon them fellows were?"

"That, Sammy, is what we want to know." Quint shook his hand, "You've been a real help, man. I'm going to give you my card. If you or your friends remember anything else, find a policeman and give him my card. Tell him to send for me, even if you think it might not be important."

"Hell. I fought for this country once. If I was worth a damn I still would. Anything I can do to help, you just let me know."

Buster reached out and shook Sammy's hand, "We'll do that. You need us to help you get moved back, or would you like us to see if we can get you some housing?"

"I don't want no housing. Like I said over yonder in the cemetery I've got a roof over my head and no rent, no utilities, no nothing. I live free as a bird. I got a mailbox where I pick up my government disability check, and it gives me enough to eat and warm clothes when I'm cold. I'm good."

Quint reached in his pocket, withdrew his wallet, and handed the man a $100 bill, "Have a steak on me."

Following suit, Buster extracted another hundred from his wallet and silently handed it to Sammy.

"Lord help me, that is mighty decent of you fellows. I mightily appreciate it. I shore do."

Chapter 12

It was a beautiful day…the sun sparkled on the river, birds were singing, and a light breeze freshened the air, but Sammy was too tired to notice. He had spent most of the day moving his belongings back to the cemetery. One more trip, and he would be finished. He trudged across the road to his spot by the bridge noting with disgust that his fellow vagrants had left their trash behind. That rankled Sammy. This was the Capital of the country he had fought for, had shed blood for, and he was angered by those who showed disrespect. Despite an old injury in his back that nagged him from time to time, he delayed getting the rest of his things to pick up the litter.

There was no waste receptacle anywhere that he could see. Sammy sighed and began to pick through the junk until he found a plastic bag that would hold most of it. The rest he stuffed in his pockets and under his shirt. He stooped under the weight of the bag. The weight of the trash was almost too much by itself, but he did not want to make a separate trip, so he also heaved up the knapsack that held his clothes. At least his neighbors by the river had not seen fit to rob him. He would not have been surprised if they had. They were a sorry lot in his mind. Now if he could just find a trash bin, he could rid himself of that and make his way back to his cemetery campsite.

Just as he began to scramble up the embankment, he heard

the steady drone of an engine. Looking up, he could see a midsized motorboat coming towards him. As the boat came closer, he could make out what appeared to be the two men that had launched the attack on the cemetery. Sammy wondered what they were up to now. Whatever it was, it did not look good. One of the men pointed his way. Seeing a gun in the man's hand, Sammy realized he was the target. Dropping his knapsack and the bag of trash, he began to run at a crouch. If he could make it to the trees, he would be able to hide in the cemetery until he could get to Quint Cord and warn him the men were back. At the top of the bank, Sammy paused to catch his breath. It was a mistake.

The men on the boat watched as a group of cyclists pedaled towards the fallen man. The first cyclist stopped. The others halted beside him. For a moment, they stood astride their bikes staring at the man on the grass.

One of the men on the boat called out, "Hey, we just heard a couple of shots? Is the old guy dead?"

The lead biker, a guy named Joe, replied, "If he's not, he's bad hit. He's bleeding like mad. I'm calling for an ambulance to see if we can save him."

The men on the boat looked at one another. They had no choice but to delay their plan and decamp as quickly as possible before the police showed up and started asking questions. Again, the man called out, "Hey, we have to go. We would hang around to see if we could be of any use, but we didn't see anything so it wouldn't help much."

With that announcement, they quickly reversed their engine and began to move back down the river. Behind them, the cyclists had surrounded Sammy, and one began applying pressure to the gaping hole in his chest. By the time an ambulance arrived, the motorboat was nearly out of sight. In the distance, an ambulance siren was echoed by those of police cars speeding to the site with blue lights flashing.

Sammy had not moved. He had lost a lot of blood. His pulse was rapid and his breathing shallow. The EMT's wasted no time hooking him up to oxygen and an IV before getting him into the ambulance. The cyclists watched as the ambulance drove away and two squad cars took its place.

The police officer in the first car got out and walked over to Joe who stood ahead of the others, "What's going on here?"

"I am sorry officer. We were cycling along the road when we spotted this old guy lying on the roadside. He had apparently been shot. We tried to help him by stopping the bleeding while we waited for an ambulance."

"Did you see who shot him?"

"No. He was already hit when we arrived."

"Did you see anyone else when you got here?"

"Yeah. There were two guys on an inboard boat. They said they heard two shots, and wanted to know if the old guy was okay."

The policeman turned to scan the river, "So what the hell happened to them?"

"They left, said they had to be somewhere, and they didn't know anything more than hearing the shots from over there." Joe waved his hand in the direction of the river. "I don't know if the shots were from someone on the river, or on the opposite bank."

The police officer, Sargent Miller, turned to the other cyclists and asked if they could identify the origin of the shots. They all shook their heads or murmured 'no.' Sgt. Miller looked both ways on the river. "Which direction did that boat go? Did you get a name or call letters? Did you tell them they needed to stay for questioning?"

"They went down river." Joe paused and squinted in concentration, "You know, I think the ID on the boat must have been painted over, or else never had a name. The guys on the boat seemed okay. They said they had to go. I mean what else could we do, since we had no way to stop them?"

"We need all your names and addresses in case we need to contact you while we investigate this. My assistant here is going to write down your info. I want everything you can remember…about any sounds you heard, the boat, descriptions of the men on it, or anything else that you recall."

The cyclists proceeded to give the police their names and contact numbers. They said the guys on the boat might be foreign as they had an accent, maybe dark hair, but it was hard to say as they were some distance away. The boat was not a large one…white with gray trim, and a small cabin. The police continued to fish for information, but none of them had anymore to add to what they had already provided. Finished with their questioning, the cyclists departed as the police retrieve the bag with Sammy's meager possessions.

When the unresponsive Sammy arrived at the hospital, he was quickly wheeled into pre-op where he was divested of his clothing and the trash he had stuffed in his shirt and pockets. He was then hastily sponged off. As the nurse's aide began to cram his belongings into a plastic bag, a business card fell to the floor. Not expecting a tramp to have a business card, she turned it over and read the name.

"Hey, guys. This old guy has a card from a special agent to the President. Since this man has been shot, do you think we should call the name on the card or just ignore it?"

Walking over, the lead emergency room surgeon, Gary Martin took the card. "I've heard of this Quint Cord fellow. He was in the news awhile back. He's a real bad ass apparently... saved the President from assassination. I suppose it's possible this man was working for Agent Cord."

He studied it for a moment longer before saying to one of the nurses, "Go out and call the number on the card and ask for Mr. Cord. Tell him why we have his card, and that we found it on an old hobo who has been badly shot."

"Yes, sir. Right away."

With that the surgeon and his team resumed scrubbing up. Within minutes, Sammy was anesthetized and then wheeled into the operating room.

As Sammy went into surgery, Quint was talking to Lila who had now moved back to the computer lab in the basement as White House occupants assumed their normal routines. She was all but tearing her hair out in frustration.

"I have never been so at sea as I am at the moment. It's like I am looking for a needle, not just in a haystack, but in an entire field of them. First of all, I don't even know what I am looking for beyond the perpetrators of the initial emails demanding ransom. That is a dead end at this point. I haven't given up, but I sure wish I had something more to go on as that source has gone dead silent. It's possible it was just a temporary site that was immediately shut down."

"I get that." Quint responded. He mulled it over for a moment before adding, "Gerald has the CIA studying the drone we recovered for clues. I can have them get you everything they have. Do you think it might be worthwhile checking out the computerized controls of the drone launchers?"

"Maybe. Get me the info you have on that drone and the micro-controller. I will program it in and backdate to the time of the attack at the cemetery."

"That would be helpful."

Before he could say anything else, the buzzing of his phone interrupted their conversation. Quint glanced at the caller ID. "Hmm, it's the downtown hospital, All Family Medical Center. I wonder what they want."

Lila merely shrugged as she waited for him to answer. "Yes, this is Quint Cord. What's going on?"

"We just brought a gunshot victim into the emergency room. He is seriously injured. While we were prepping him for surgery, your business card fell out of his pocket. The man is elderly and judging by his clothing, poverty stricken. At this point, we do not know anything about him as there is no ID in his pocket. We wondered if you might be able to help us. Maybe, let us know if he has any next of kin."

"Is he dying?"

"We have stabilized him, but it doesn't look good."

"I'll be there shortly."

Quint hung up and looked at Lila. He shook his head as his mouth quirked into a grimace. "Dammit, I think that was about the old guy I talked to by the bridge near the cemetery, the one that told me about seeing the drones launched. He's about to go into surgery for treatment of a severe bullet wound."

"Do you think the men he saw on the barge came back looking for him?"

"That is a strong possibility. You start digging on that drone launch as soon as Gerald gets the info to you. I'll phone him on the way to the hospital."

It was not a long drive from the White House to the hospital on Rhode Island Avenue. The front desk directed him to the surgical waiting room where Quint presented his CIA badge and asked for Sammy Crenshaw saying he had received a call from the hospital and was a friend. The receptionist in the waiting area told Quint that Mr. Crenshaw was not yet out of surgery.

"Would you tell his surgeon that I need to be informed immediately of Mr. Crenshaw's status once he is out of surgery."

"Of course. I'll ask the doctor if he would like to talk to you since there are no family members here. It will have to wait until he is out of surgery." She frowned for a moment. "Do you know if Mr. Crenshaw has family that needs to be notified? Normally we do not share surgical information with non-family members."

"I don't know anything about any family members. Mr. Crenshaw has been leading a solitary life for some time. Besides, the surgeon had a nurse call me to notify me of his injury, so I assume the doctor will be willing to talk to me. Furthermore, this is a potential victim of an investigation we are conducting. That badge gives me the right to question Mr. Crenshaw the minute he is able to respond."

"I see." The receptionist shrugged and answered the phone as Quint walked over to a chair near the television.

To kill time, he pulled out his phone and began to thumb through emails. Most were junk. The others he read and, where warranted, replied to them. He shifted in the chair to find a more comfortable position. Another check of his watch assured him that only thirty minutes had elapsed since he last looked. There were few things he despised more than idle sitting. In his mind he played over the conversation he had had with Sammy while he was camped by the bridge. Nothing stood out that would make Quint think that there was a reason why Sammy and none of the others would have been shot...or had they? Wanting to ascertain whether or not that was true, Quint called the police and asked if there had been any other shooting victims in the area of the Potomac bridge adjacent to Arlington Cemetery in the last few hours.

They assured him that the only one shot was some homeless guy. When he identified himself as an agent with the CIA, they provided him with the information they had collected from the bicyclist that found Sammy. Quint thanked them and hung up. After another thirty minutes he began to pace around the waiting area. The desk receptionist glared at him even though there were few others in the area. Quint considered glaring back. Dismissing it as childish, he returned to his seat.

Retrieving his phone from his jacket pocket, Quint dialed Gerald Williams and related what he knew about his informant being shot. Gerald listened carefully to the information and then told Quint he would get an agent on the scene to go over anything the police might have missed, and he was assigning an around- the-clock guard for Sammy's room. Quint then resumed his vigil. When another hour passed, he walked up to the receptionist and asked if she could learn how much longer he might be in surgery. She shrugged with annoyance and pointed to the electronic patient board. "That," she snarled, "says he is still in surgery. I have no way of knowing how much longer. He will go to recovery and then ICU. I already let surgery know that you are waiting to talk to the doctor. That is the best I can do. There is a coffee shop down the way. Why don't you get something? If the doctor comes looking for you, I can tell him where to find you."

"I don't care for any coffee, thanks." Quint walked back to his seat and stared at the electronic board, willing it to update.

Another hour passed before Quint heard his name called and looked up to see an older man in surgical garb walking his way. Quint immediately stood and waited for the doctor.

The doctor stuck out his hand and shook Quint's. "Mr. Cord, I'm Dr. Gary Martin. I'm the one that operated on the elderly gentleman that had your card."

"Thank you, doctor. Is there somewhere we could talk privately for a few minutes?"

"Of course. The conference room is right over here." Dr. Martin pointed to a door off to one side and led the way with Quint following. Once in the room both men seated themselves at a Formica topped table.

Quint placed both hands on the table in front of him and leaned towards the doctor. "What can you tell me about Sammy's condition, and when will I be able to talk to him about what happened?"

The doctor grimaced, "I don't know what your connection is to my patient, but I assure you, the man is in no condition to deal with any questions. He is only just now out of surgery. For the moment, he is in recovery, and afterwards he will be transferred to intensive care. When he is alert and stable, you will be able to talk to him. I have your card and can call you when I feel he is up to it."

"I understand and sympathize with your caution; however I need to talk to him as soon as possible. I cannot discuss details, but it is possible that Sammy was shot because he discovered something about the recent attack on the President at his wife's funeral."

"Oh, yes. What a terrible thing that was. I watched some of the news footage on television. Some of the injured are still hospitalized here." Doctor Martin paused, "I will let you talk to Sammy once he is alert, but only for a few minutes. He's lucky to be alive, and he is going to need time to recover from his injuries. I don't want him unduly upset."

"I understand. I will not push him or stay long enough to tire him."

"I appreciate the urgency, but it will be hours yet before he's alert. It's late. Why don't you go home? I will call you when he is up to answering a few questions."

Frustrated but understanding the doctor's position, Quint stood and shook his hand. "Thanks for meeting with me. I'll be waiting for your call."

CHAPTER 13

As Quint walked into the White House, he was troubled. Something just did not feel right. True, a Russian or Russians were probably involved in Dianna's kidnapping. But why would North Korea, Russia, China, plus Iran, so defy international norms as to attack the President and his family and demand an end to NATO and the US's threatened sanctions if they proceeded with the proposed nuclear arms deal? Certainly, that was a worrisome prospect, but were those countries behind the recent attacks? Normally, such things were handled with threats and saber rattling on both sides until reaching a compromise. If they had taken it to the level of a personal attack on the leader of the free world and his family, they would face the wrath of the UN and most of the countries on Earth. Were they really that brazen, or was some other operative or operatives to blame?

The President and Gerald Williams were convinced that it was a cabal of Russia, China, North Korea, and possibly Iran, hoping to change the policy of the United States towards the four nations entering into an agreement on the development and sharing of nuclear weapons and technology. The problem was finding the connection between those who kidnapped Dianna, killed the First Lady, and the two foreigners who launched killer drones at her funeral; and then tying those events to the instigators. So far, despite extensive poking around in the ethernet for bad operatives that could have been involved, Lila had found nothing, nor had the CIA. They would continue to go down rabbit holes in hopes of finding something. For Quint, there were several angles he wanted to pursue to find answers. How many individuals could be tied to Dianna? If they had found Barbara Rhodes' phone, had they checked incoming and outgoing calls, and where did that lead? Could they find any DNA on the burned body of the kidnapper and if so, could they ID the man? If they could ID him, was he tied to others? Was his telephone not so badly burned that they could retrieve the chip? Was there any way to check the car to see if it was rented or registered to some individual or entity that was not rental? Had the license plate melted, or if not, were the raised letters still readable even with the paint burned off? Was the bomb in the hospital planted by an employee, someone with the security forces, or an unknown suspect? Were the foreigners on the barge a part of a cabal or were they acting on their own? If part of a cabal, who was behind it…a foreign country, countries, or individuals with an unknown motive? Frustrated with the lack of answers, Quint turned the possibilities over and over in his mind. He could not just sit back and wait. It was time to get things moving before any clues were lost.

Quint texted his questions to Gerald Williams as his CIA agents should have already been digging into some of those questions. He then sent a copy to Lila and Buster. Buster immediately texted back that he was on the way to the cabin to search both it and the woods along the path Barbara and her pursuer had followed. He was taking a metal detector with him to help with the search. Buster copied his text to Quint to both Lila and Gerald Williams.

Quint was familiar with the metal detector that Buster

favored. It was a German made OKM model EXP 6000 designed to penetrate various surfaces with considerable accuracy. If Barbara's phone was out there, Buster would find it. With the phone, they should be able to get the phone company to provide access to the call log. That could be a big break into at least one component of the puzzle.

Entering the guest suite they had been assigned, Quint looked around for his wife. Not finding her in the sitting area or bedroom, he walked into the bathroom steamy from the shower that sluiced hot water over his wife's body. He admired the view through the fogged over shower door for a moment. What the heck, he decided. Quickly he removed his clothes and dropped them haphazardly on the tile floor before opening the door and stepping in beside his wife.

She gasped, "I didn't know you were back."

"I just got here, and I was distracted when I saw you in here."

He rubbed his hands over her body, "Are you distracted is the question?"

"Oh, no. I am very focused. Let's dry off and take this to the bedroom."

Twenty minutes later, Quint rolled over in bed and took her in his arms. "You are a wonder, and I am so thankful we are married."

"So am I." Lisa kissed him on the shoulder. "What brought you home?"

"I'm not comfortable with the direction of this investigation. Something about it is off kilter."

"What's the problem?"

"What if the countries we have assumed are behind this are not the real culprits?"

"But what other reason could there be than stopping the nuclear agreement?"

"I suspect that is the real question. If Russia, China, North Korea, and Iran are not behind it, who is? There are too many loose ends that we need to tie together. I called Gerald, and the CIA is going to try a few new angles. I want you to look again at Dianna's phone. Check the number that she called for Barb. Can you hack into that or find out who it was registered to and what other calls were made by Barb to other individuals?"

"Short answer, no. Phone protocol from these providers does not allow the government to do that without major paperwork. It would be easier if I had Barbara's phone. Then I can hack into that and pull the numbers she called. But we don't have it."

"Buster is out looking for it now. I'm hoping she dropped it in the woods at some point before she was murdered. He may find Dianna's, too."

"Hopefully, if he finds Barbara's it will give us a lead into who kidnapped Dianna…provided I can hack in and then identify the numbers she called and that called her."

"Exactly. That would give us one piece of the puzzle, but I think there are a lot more pieces. Let's assume they are Russian as we suspect. I am hoping Sammy can tell me something more about the men on the boat as soon as the doctor allows me in to talk to him."

"There's not much more we can do until you hear from Buster, Sammy, or Gerald." Lila shrugged. "Besides, I've worked up an appetite. Let's have dinner. The chef here is something else. I think Teresa would be jealous, so be sure not to brag on him." Quint laughed, "I know better than that. Come on. Let's see what's for dinner."

After dinner they returned to their suite and turned on the news. Not much was of interest, but they cuddled on the sofa as they watched. Cord curled up at their feet and was soon snoring softly. Quint had almost nodded off when his phone rang.

"Gerald, what's up?"

"Buster just brought us the phone that he found in the woods not far from where we found Barbara's body. He also found one not too far from the wreck site. It is undamaged so we assume it was thrown from the car when it rolled. Not only that, but we found Dianna's as well. It had been tossed into the woods not far from the cabin. It probably won't give us much, but once we are done with it. She can have it back."

"That's great. When will we get them over here?"

"Forensics is checking them over for fingerprints. As soon as they are finished, I will take them to Lila. If she can hack in, we may just get a break in this case. The two from Barbara and the dead guy appear to be Burner Phones."

"We need a break. The whole thing is one strange can of worms. I can't help thinking we are on the wrong track."

An hour later, his phone rang again. Rolling over, Quint picked it up from the bedside table. Clearing the grogginess of sleep from his throat, he answered, "Gerald, do you have something?"

"We ran the fingerprints on the phone of the guy that died in the crash. They match those of a Russian thug that we have monitored for the last couple of years. He is anyone's bird dog. Goes by the name of Ivan Smirnov. He also used the name Ivan Sidorav. The fingerprints of the girl known as Barbara Rhodes are those of Lena Zakharova who came here several years ago with her parents. They appear to have slipped in illegally from

Canada. The only thing we have on her is a charge for shoplifting that was eventually dropped. We do not know of any tie between the two, other than their Russian births. We are going to bring the Zakharov family in for questioning to see what they know. I will also have to tell the Zakharovs that their daughter is dead. No doubt they will want to claim the body from the morgue."

"Are you through with the forensics on the phones? I know Lila is anxious to get a crack at them."

"She will have them first thing in the morning. Now, let's all get a good night's sleep."

"Thanks, Gerald. Goodnight."

Lila sat up on one elbow, "Good news?"

"You will have two phones tomorrow, plus Dianna's. Dianna can give you the password for hers. Let's hope you can hack into the other two. Gerald has the names of the owners for you, but not much else."

Lila murmured a sleepy "Hmm," before rolling over and falling back asleep. For Quint sleep was a long time coming. Sometime after two in the morning he drifted off into a fitful slumber. He was awakened at 5:00 by the persistent ringing of his phone. In his befuddled state it took him a moment to find it and murmur, "Yeah?"

"Mr. Cord, this is the charge nurse at All Family Medical Center. Sammy Crenshaw is awake and calling for you. I tried to calm him down, but he's very agitated. He says he needs to talk to you right away. I hate to ask at this hour, but is it possible for you to come to the hospital? It is not good for him to be this worked up."

"I'll be there. Tell him I'm on the way. In the meantime, make sure the security detail outside his room is on high alert."

"I'll do that."

Lila rolled over and touched Quint on the shoulder and asked, "What time is it? Who was that?"

"It's early, sweetheart. Go back to sleep. Sammy is awake and asking for me. I need to go."

Lila sleepily murmured an okay before rolling over and going back to sleep. Quint quietly dressed and then walked over and kissed her lightly on the forehead. He patted Cord who had followed him to the door before letting himself out.

At the front entrance to the White House, he requested a car and driver which was immediately brought to him. Thirty minutes after the call, Quint was at the hospital. He wasted no time in hurrying to Sammy's room. When the elevator arrived at the third floor, Quint walked off. The security guard was standing outside of Sammy's door with his hand inside the front of his coat. Quint assumed it was on his weapon.

Walking up to him, Quint inquired, "What's going on?"

"The old guy says someone is going to kill him so he can't talk. Says they already tried once. I'm not taking any chances on him having a heart attack or something. I hope you can calm him down."

"Sammy may be right. He saw the guys that attacked the First Lady's funeral. I suspect they came back and shot him to keep him from talking." Quint could hear Sammy's shouts from the hall. The man was for sure worked up.

"Shit! I had no idea I was assigned to protect someone this toxic to the bad guys."

Quint was instantly annoyed, "Why the hell do you think you were assigned to a protection detail? If someone were not a threat to him, do you think he would need protection?"

The guard hung his head. "I'm sorry. I know that. It's just that my wife is due to go into labor any minute. I need to be with her. That's a lot more important to me than this job."

Regretting the angry remark, Quint replied, "Hey, man, I get it. I'm sorry I barked at you. I would feel the same way in your shoes. I'll call the Agency and have them send someone else to cover for you."

The guard lifted his head. "Thanks. I would really appreciate that."

"Sure." Quint turned from the guard and opened the door. Sammy looked like hell. Tubes were running everywhere; and Sammy was sitting up in bed pulling against the restraints that held him in place. "Sammy, calm down before you hurt yourself. I'm here, and I'm going to see you are safe."

Sammy lay back on the pillow, "Thank God. I am so glad you are here. Those SOBs tried to kill me."

"Who tried to kill you?"

"Those same guys I saw on the barge when the funeral was attacked."

"Are you sure?"

"Yeah, dammit, I'm sure. Why the hell do you think I am lying here all shot up?"

Quint took his hand, careful to avoid disturbing the IV line. "Okay, Sammy. Now try to calm down and tell me what happened."

Sammy looked at the door to be sure it was closed before speaking. "I went back to the site by the river to collect my stuff so I could move back to the cemetery. I looked up on my last trip up the embankment and saw this inboard motorboat coming straight at me. Looked like the same two guys on it I saw on the boat with the drones. They saw me spot them and that's the last thing I knew until I woke up here."

"Tell me everything you can remember before they shot you."

"Like I told you before they were sorta foreign looking. I didn't like the way the boat was aiming straight at me. I figured they were up to no good, and I scrambled up the bank to get away because I knew they had seen me looking at them both times."

"What do you remember of the boat? Did you see the boat ID, the features of the two men, anything that might help us?"

"The first two numbers on the hull were 689. I can't remember the others. I just suspect they shot me because they think I can identify them. They ain't stupid. I bet they are checking hospitals right now to find the latest gunshot victims. If they come here, I'm a dead man because I know what they look like."

"Sammy, we have an armed guard outside your door and there is another on the stairs leading up, and another in the lobby. We are going to do our best to keep you safe."

"If I'm so safe, how did I end up here all shot up?"

"No one foresaw that, or you would have been under protection sooner. It is the government's fault. My fault for that matter. I would never have knowingly exposed you to danger."

"Look, I know there ain't nothing deliberate here. But fact is I'm all shot up and there are folks that want me dead."

"Sammy, I realize the jeopardy that you are in. I will do my best to keep you safe. I want you to trust me to do that. What I need now is for you to try to remember exactly what you saw and describe it to me in the smallest detail even if you think it is unimportant. Can you do that?"

"Yeah. I'll try. I was getting my stuff and had about finished, but there was a bunch of trash that needed cleaning up, so it was taking me a while. I was just about wore slam out on that last climb up the riverbank. That's when I saw them fellers on the boat. I began to get out of there as fast as I could because I saw one of them point at me." Sammy paused.

"So, what happened then?"

"That's when they shot me. I don't remember nothing after that until I woke up here this morning. It's morning ain't it?"

"Yes, Sammy. It's a little after six." Quint leaned forward and asked, "Sammy, let's assume they shot you deliberately because they remembered you from the attack on the funeral. I really need to know anything you can tell me about the barge or boat, and what you can remember about the two men. It might not only help us find them and stop them before further attacks, but it is important to helping us keep you safe."

CHAPTER 14

Dianna and Lila began pouring over her phone as soon as the CIA turned it over. As Quint had suspected, other than a couple of innocuous calls between her and Barb, there was nothing useful. After Dianna left with her reclaimed phone, Lila picked up Barbara's phone. Using clues as to possible passwords that Dianna had provided, Lila soon logged into Barbara's phone and began a search of the call history. The last few were made to a phone in the Alexandria area code. A search of the number came up empty. She suspected she was calling either a Burner Phone, or a throw away phone deliberately purchased to be untraceable.

Lila began working on the phone from the man that died in the crash, Ivan Smirnov. Although his phone was a Burner Phone, perhaps he called numbers that were not. Her first job was to try to hack into the phone. After an hour, she silently swore. The man had installed Phoner to effectively shield his calls and texts. That made her job of tracking his cellular activity much harder.

At the hospital, Sammy had calmed down enough that Quint removed his restraints and elevated the head of his bed to make him more comfortable. Sammy had just finished describing how the two foreigners on the barge had returned in a boat and shot at him when Quint jerked his head up. His nerve endings began tingling on high alert. He grabbed his gun and flipped off the safety before rolling Sammy's bed into the corner. If someone out there wanted in that was not on the hospital staff, Quint would know why first. Waiting beside the door, he watched the lever handle turn down as a hand on the door frame began to slowly push it open. Not hesitating, Quint grabbed the hand and jerked. Thrown off balance, the other man began to stagger into the room before recovering himself. With pistol drawn and cocked, Quint snarled, "Who the hell are you?"

The man swung at him, striking Quint on the shoulder holding the gun. It dropped slightly, give the other man a chance to turn his own gun toward Quint. Lunging forward, Quint knocked the man's gun away. The man then lunged at Quint grabbing him around the waist and knocking him to the floor with the assailant on top. Both men began trading vicious punches in a fight to the death.

Sammy watched helplessly from the bed realizing that if Quint lost, he was a dead man. He searched the objects on his bedside table and found nothing he could use as a weapon. Not one to go down without a fight, his wartime training kicked in as he watched the invader getting the upper hand. Ignoring the tubes connected to him and his own weakened state, he rolled from the bed onto the floor. Using one of the plastic tubes, he managed to loop it around the attacker's neck and pull with all the strength he had left. As the man struggled to loosen the noose like tube, Quint was freed to join his own strength to Sammy's. Quint watched as the man's grip weakened and he stopped struggling.

Sammy groaned, "I never thought I would have to do that again, but I didn't think I had a choice. He had at least forty pounds on you and looked to be as strong as a bull."

Quint sat up wincing as he did so. He was bleeding from various cuts. Exploring his mouth with his tongue, he was relieved no teeth felt loosened despite several blows that were already making themselves felt as the adrenalin rush subsided. "Thanks, man. That was not going so well."

Reaching over Quint grabbed the nurse call on the side of the bed. Despite pain screaming at him from multiple points, he helped Sammy back into the bed. With all the monitors beeping, he could not understand why a nurse had not already come to check on the patient.

"Where in the hell are the nurses when you need them?"

"They for sure are all over me when I don't want them."

Quint squatted on the floor beside the unknown assailant and felt for his pulse.

"Is he dead?"

"He appears to be. I don't get any pulse. In a way that is too bad as I would love to know who sent him to kill you. By the way, was he one of the men on the boat?"

"Never saw him before." Sammy shook his head, "Good grief. I never thought I would see the day I would be in as much danger as I was in Nam."

"If you are okay, I'm going to see if I can find a nurse to stop that damned machine from squawking."

"Yeah, I'm tough. Go on and find a nurse."

Quint patted Sammy on the shoulder. "Hang in there. I'll be right back."

As Quint turned to walk out the door, he remembered the security agent that had wanted to get home to his wife. He did not have long to wonder what happened to him. Just outside the door, the man was curled up on the floor with blood pouring from a wound in his upper chest. Quint crouched beside him and felt for a pulse. It was there but faint. Pressing on the wound to stop the bleeding, Quint shouted for help. Quint pushed from his mind the urgency in the agent's face when he said he wanted to get home to his wife who was about to go into labor. There was no time to dwell on regrets and sympathy. When he had no answer to his call for help, he shook the agent and asked, "Can you hear me?"

The agent groaned, opened his eyes, and croaked, "Yeah."

"Listen to me. I need to get help for you. I am going to put your hand over your wound. Even if it hurts, you need to press as hard as you can. Can you do that?"

"I'll try."

"Good man. Someone is going to fix you up so you can get home to that wife of yours before she has that baby. Remember that and hold on."

The agent gave a weak smile and nodded. "Hurry. My wife…"

"Don't worry. Someone will let her know."

Quint stood and looked around the hall. No one else seemed to be about. Walking down the hall to the nurses' station, he saw that it was devoid of anyone. At that point, he heard a banging on a door further down on the left. Hurrying to it, he leaned into the door and shouted, "Can you hear me?"

"Yes! Get us out of here. That man with the gun locked us in here and took the key. There is another key in the nurses' station. Look in the drawer under the first computer and you will see it. It's the one with a blue tag."

"Got it. I'll be right back."

Quint hurried to retrieve the key and insert it into the storage closet door. Three nurses were huddled inside. Their eyes round with fright, the oldest of them asked, "What in the hell is going on?"

"I need your help. We have an injured CIA agent in the hall and Sammy's monitors are screaming. We need a doctor up here fast."

The nurses ran down the hall. The oldest one reached the agent and took over applying pressure. The second rushed to Sammy's room. The third began paging doctors and security to come to the third floor. With the three nurses and a doctor taking care of the medical urgencies, Quint called Gerald.

He glanced at his watch as Gerald's phone rang. It was seven in the morning. A lot had happened in a short time. Gerald sounded sleepy when he answered. "Yeah, Quint. What's up."

"Someone just tried to kill Sammy. I stopped him, and whoever it was is dead. Sammy's okay, but the guard you assigned is badly wounded. His wife is about to go into labor. Please have someone go in person to let his wife know what has happened."

"No problem. Anyone else?"

"I have not checked the access points to see who else is down, but if you covered stairwells and elevator access, I suspect they've been hit, too."

"Dammit. I'm on the way. I'll call for immediate backup. Let me know what else you learn."

"Right."

Quint hung up and walked toward the stairwell. He would check it first. There should have been someone assigned to each of the levels, counting from the basement. Next, he would check the elevator on the lowest floor and work his way up. Walking down the stairs to the second landing, Quint spotted blood sprayed on the wall before he saw the body lying just inside the access door. He quickly checked to see if the man was alive. Shaking his head, he hurried down to the first-floor landing. The agent there was lying on the bottom step. Judging by the angle of his neck, Quint figured it had been snapped killing the man instantly. Continuing down to the basement, he suspected he would find another dead agent on the lower level. As expected, the third agent's body was lying against the wall. Judging by the wounds, the man had fought bravely prior to being shot. Whoever had done the killings was a professional assassin judging by the bodies. He would have used a silencer when he shot three of the agents. Quint surmised he sneaked up behind the one whose neck was broken and killed him before he could react. Exiting the stairwell on the lowest level, he walked over to the elevator. He saw nobody in the surrounding area. Pushing the button to call the elevator, he watched as the numbers above the door counted down from two. When the doors slid open, he entered and was relieved to see no body on the floor. The walls were clean of blood or any sign of struggle. At the first level, he stopped, held his hand on the door to hold the elevator, and checked the immediate area. The agent there was leaning casually against the wall.

Quint flashed his badge. "Hey, why don't we have someone assigned to the lower level?"

"We do. He told me he was going to the bathroom. I've not seen him since."

"Can you describe him to me?"

"Sure. He seemed like a nice guy. I don't think I ever met him, but no surprise there. A lot of guys work for the agency. He was a big guy, maybe six three or four, probably two hundred or more pounds. Clean shaven, slightly balding. Nothing special looking. Just ordinary other than being tall. Why? What's up?"

"I think he may have been a hired killer. We have three dead agents in the stairwells, and one badly injured on the third floor. The killer is dead, too."

"Dammit! What in the hell happened?"

"I suspect it has to do with the attack on the funeral when the First Lady was buried. The guy that was a witness to the drone launch is the one you are assigned to protect. I just prevented him from being added to the body count. I think you are lucky you were not shot."

"This is the most public location, so I doubt he wanted to start here. He probably went to the basement and started from there. Any idea who he replaced?"

"No clue. The Director is on his way. Hopefully, he will be able to answer some of the questions."

Forty-five minutes later, Gerald Williams exited the elevator with a grim countenance. He was accompanied by four equally grim looking men and a woman that Quint knew from previous visits to the Agency. He walked up to them, "I'm glad you're here, Director. Hopefully, you can answer some questions."

"First things first. I'm having Sammy Crenshaw transferred to a top-secret location with around the clock guards and a private nursing staff. They are all thoroughly vetted, and I trust them." Gerald turned and pointed to the room, "Okay guys, you know what to do."

The oldest of the men, nodded, "Yes, sir. We're on it."

Gerald waited until they went into Sammy's room to initiate

the relocation. "I already alerted the staff here to prep Sammy to be moved."

"It certainly seems like the best option." Quint indicated a conference room down the hall. "Perhaps, we should make use of it for our talk."

Gerald followed Quint to the door in question. Quint opened the door and finding it empty they entered and flipped the occupied sign on the door. Once both men had seated themselves at the conference table, Gerald began, "The three dead agents were those assigned to this detail. The lead agent is the man you spoke to in the lobby. It appears the man assigned to the lower level was killed and replaced by the assassin. I have a forensics team on the way to collect the bodies of my agents and that of the killer. I am hoping he is on our watch list, and we get a quick ID."

"I would love to know how they knew Sammy was here."

"Good question. At this point, I don't know any more than you do. I can only surmise we have a leak at the Agency or they were monitoring police phones. I am having a re-vetting done of every person on the staff there, as well as the agents assigned here. I am hoping something turns up so we can nip that problem in the bud. It might also explain how they were able to plant the bomb on the floor outside of Diana Northrup's room."

"We need a break of some kind before this gets worse."

"Speaking of worse, you definitely look the worse for wear. You have a couple of cuts on your face that are oozing blood, and a lump on your head. Do we need to have a doctor check you?"

"It's nothing. Just a result of tangling with the killer.

Fortunately, Sammy jumped in to help me, otherwise you might have another couple of bodies on your hands...mine and Sammy's."

"Good for Sammy. He sounds like one tough old geezer."

"Trust me, he is." Quint paused, "Do I need to know where Sammy is being relocated?"

Gerald looked down at the table. "Maybe, maybe not. You have some kind of rapport established with the man?"

"I do. He trusts me."

"Good enough." Gerald proceeded to explain where Sammy was going to be held.

"Another thing I've been running over in my mind is the possibility that Sammy just ended up in the wrong place at the wrong time when he was shot. Suppose they were returning to the same place they launched the drones for some other purpose, saw Sammy, recognized him from the drone attack, and decided to take him out as a witness to whatever they were up to. If that's the case, they could be going back to the area where he was shot for some further plan they have in mind."

"Those are good points. I will have a detail assigned to watch the area immediately. Either way, Sammy is still in danger as a witness who could possibly identify them."

CHAPTER 15

Lila was smiling when Quint returned to the White House lab where she was hunched over her computer keyboard apparently in deep contemplation. Giving her a kiss on the forehead, he sat in the chair beside her and asked, "What is my favorite wife so concentrated on?"

"You mean your only one!" Lila laughed before adding, "As for the concentration, I have nailed one perp. Ivan Sidorav, AKA Ivan Smirnov, is the only one Barbara Rhodes called on her phone other than her parents and Dianna. I think we can assume Ivan was her immediate handler. Using CIA Geo Spatial tracking software, I was able to break into Sidorav's phone despite the 128 bit encryptions. If I triangulate his location, most of his calls were from Alexandria and were made to another phone in a nearby location. I am trying to zero in on that now. I am also going to try to hack into the phone he called there to see what I can learn."

"I don't know how you do it," Quint said. "I'm continually awed by your expertise."

"I don't have the means as a private citizen. The CIA is letting me use their top-secret software. I cannot even tell you what it is, but trust me, this stuff is phenomenal in terms of what it can do. It still takes some patient digging, but I think I'm going to get there. I'm hoping the program I'm running will give me some results by tomorrow."

"Knowing you if it can be done you will. Let me know what you come up with."

"Always." Lila turned to look at Quint for the first time. "What in the hell have you been up to? You're scabbed, there are blood smears on your clothes, and a huge lump on your forehead."

Quint shrugged, "It's nothing. I had a little run-in with a bad guy."

"It doesn't look like nothing." Lila pushed back from her computer and stood, worry evident in her face. "This will keep a few minutes more. Let's go up and see if we can get you patched up and into some clean clothes. You can tell me what happened while I take care of the mess you made of yourself." Pausing, she looked more closely at the wounds on his face and arms, "Are you sure you don't need stitches?"

"No. I'm okay. The doctor checked me before I left. It's all surface," Quint crossed his fingers behind his back at the lie. He knew she would be livid that he had not had a doctor check him out once she saw the full extent of his injuries.

Lila shook her head. Her eyes narrowed at him, she remarked, "I hope you think I buy that, tough guy!"

"Come on, it's nothing. I'm fine. I won't tell you that I don't have a few aches and pains, but it's no big deal. I'm not stupid. If I needed medical treatment, I would get it. I have dealt with much worse."

"Not since I've known you!" Lila glared, "Okay, tough guy, let's get those wounds cleaned and bandaged."

Offering no fruitless argument, Quint followed her to the elevator that would take them from the basement to their suite. He felt like hell and was second guessing his decision not to have the lump on his head checked out. He just hoped there was no major concussion going on. He did not have time to deal with down time. There was too much at stake. Unless they found the people behind the recent events, things could become much worse.

In the bathroom of their suite, Quint winced as Lila methodically dabbed alcohol on his wounds. His head was throbbing enough without the additional pain.

Lila studied him for a moment. "Quint, look at me." Reluctantly he looked up and stared into her eyes.

"We are calling the doctor on staff right now. One of your pupils is more dilated than the other. I'm no doctor, but I think you have a concussion."

Hurting too badly to care Quint shrugged, "Okay, let's get it over with. We've got too much to do."

"I know, Quint. But you are no help if you are unwell."

An hour later per the White House staff doctor's orders, Quint was in an ambulance headed back to the hospital where he had just left Sammy. He wasn't happy, but between the doctor and Lila he had been given no choice but to go for a scan to see what was going on inside his skull. The pounding headache left him little energy to argue. Despite his tough front, he was beginning to worry that his injury was worse than he had pretended. Every time he tried to close his eyes, either Lila or the EMT shook him with a warning to stay awake. As far as he was concerned, sleep would be a welcome oblivion from the throbbing pain.

After enduring the battery of tests and the CT scan ordered by the emergency room doctors, Quint was admitted to the hospital. When he was settled in his room, the doctor walked in. Anxious for the results of his tests, both Lila and Quint looked at him. Both heaved a sigh of relief when the doctor smiled.

"I don't think we have met Mr. Cord. I'm Dr. Robert Frazier. The White House physician is a friend of mine. He called and asked me to handle your case. After running the tests, I am happy to tell you that you're a lucky man. You have a couple of cracked ribs that are going to trouble you a little but they will heal. Although the concussion is not serious, it is imperative that you take it easy the next few days. We are keeping you here overnight for observation as a normal precaution. If you do well tonight and develop no other symptoms, we may be able to release you tomorrow. I've ordered a pain killer for the headache. The main thing is for you to keep to the minimum of mental and physical stimulation for the next few days to give your brain time to heal from the trauma. Once the headache subsides, you should be able to resume normal activities. That means no computers, no business calls, nothing that requires any serious mental activity until then. Soft music and calming movies are okay. You are encouraged to get up and walk when you feel like it, but slowly. You are not out to compete in a marathon. That's pretty much it. Do you have any questions?"

Quint shrugged, "You've summed it up pretty well, but the timing is terrible. I have too much to do and too little time to do it. I am trying to find who is behind the attacks on the President and his family. Who knows what else could be in the works."

"I was informed of the urgency of your research; however, I am sure there are others who can be assigned to work on the case while you are out of commission. If you want to fully recover, you remember what I said. Take it easy. You could cause serious problems down the road if you do not."

Lila glanced over at Quint, "Don't worry, doctor. Whether he likes it or not, he will do what you say, or I will give him worse than a concussion to worry about."

"Great. Two against one," Quint lamented. Quint studied his clasped hands. He was smart enough to realize he had little choice but to listen to the doctor.

The doctor patted him on the shoulder, "Why don't the three of us unite in getting you well as soon as possible?"

"Okay, Dr. Frazier. I'll behave since you two leave me no choice. But you need to get me out of here the minute you think I am even close to ready."

"Anxiety and fretting about the enforced inactivity are not going to help you heal. Try to relax and not think about your job."

After the doctor left, his nurse came in with something to relieve Quint's headache. That was the one thing Quint really wanted. He smiled and thanked her after she administered the shot to his rump. Lila held his hand while they waited for the medicine to take effect. After a few minutes, she asked, "How are you doing?"

Quint grimaced before growling, "The medicine helps. The headache is only a small throb, nothing like what it was. I can stand this. And don't worry. I realize I have no choice but to do what the doctor says. In the meantime, call Gerald and let him know I am out of commission for a few days." Quint closed his eyes, drowsy as the drug began to take effect.

"I'll do that. Now, stop worrying about anything and get well." Lila leaned over and kissed him on the forehead. "I'm going back to work now. I'll be back up later. You rest. That's an order."

Catching her hand, Quint opened his eyes and smiled. "I love you Mrs. Cord."

"I love you, too, Mr. Cord. Now behave yourself. I don't like sleeping alone."

Despite Dr. Frazier's promise, Quint was not discharged the following day. For the next three days, Quint could do nothing but twiddle his thumbs in irritation at the enforced inactivity. Deep in his gut, he knew the investigation into the kidnapping of the President's daughter and the murder of his wife were on the wrong track. Forbidden to dwell on the questions that were left unanswered, Quint forced himself to follow doctor's orders. Lila's ever watchful eyes were not the only ones assuring his compliance. When she left for the office in the White House basement, a stream of casual visitors replaced her surveillance. From the hospital staff to the Secret Service agents, he rarely had a moment alone. He even started to jokingly ask if anyone wanted to accompany him to the bathroom to take care of bodily demands. All he got was smiles and stoicism. Nothing was moving any of them from the watch detail. The doctor's daily visit to check on him amounted to nothing but a "soon" when Quint questioned him about a return to work. By the fourth day, he awakened without a headache and a determination to get back to work. Not wasting a moment, he called the doctor's private number and told him that the headache had gone. Not satisfied with that alone, Frazier asked him to wait for the hospital to do a follow-up MRI. Several hours later, following positive results from the test, Quint left the hospital in the Secret Service car that had taken him there.

Quint turned to the Secret Service agent, "Can you drive me to CIA headquarters, or do I need to return to the White House for my car?"

"No problem, sir. I'm your ride for the day. The Director assigned me to drive you for the next couple of days." The agent turned and grinned at his passenger. "You are one eager beaver for a newly recovered man."

"You don't even know. There are some serious things going down, and if we don't find out who is behind this shit-storm, who knows what will happen next."

Quint called Gerald Williams to let him know he was on the way. It was pushing the end of the office day, but he knew Gerald would wait. Next, he called Lila to let her know he was stopping by the CIA headquarters at Langley on the way back to the White House. Disappointingly, she had nothing new in her attempt to track the perpetrators. For the remainder of the ride, Quint was quiet. Despite telling the doctor he was fine, and the scan showing no lingering problem, Quint's prolonged inactivity left him feeling tired. He promised himself a long walk on the White House grounds with Code as soon as he finished debriefing Gerald.

"The Russian Vlad Zahrazhin. Does that ring a bell?" Gerald didn't waste any time getting down to business. He waved Quint over to a chair in front of his littered desk.

Quint settled back into the deep leather chair, "Wasn't he the one implicated in an assassination attempt in England last year? Best I remember, he was not prosecuted due to lack of evidence."

"That's the one. We have reason to believe he is in the D.C. area. I have asked Lila to see if he had any connection to either Ivan Sidorav, AKA Ivan Smirnov, or Lena Zakharova, whom we know as Barbara Rhodes. Why he would be here and what he is up to we don't know. However, he is one shady character with a long list of international charges he has managed to escape. I also have assets checking with Interpol to locate his address which is a farfetched wish, and any affiliations that might turn up in past charges. They suspect he is a highly paid hitman and espionage agent.

"I want to know who is controlling him and if there are any others, as yet unidentified, that are out there looking to cause trouble by using his expertise. I have a deep in my gut feeling this is not some kind cabal of our Country's enemies, but some nefarious organization out to get the President out of office."

"If that's the case, why not wait for the next election? It's a little less than a year away."

"According to the latest polling, the murder of the First Lady and Dianna's kidnapping actually saw a huge upswing in the President's favor. If they are trying to cost him the next election, this is not the way to do it."

"That still does not explain Dianna's ransom note demanding that he back down on the nuclear armament deal."

Quint was silent for a moment as he reached up and scratched his head. An idea began to form, and he waited for it to gel before speaking. "Gerald let's assume it is about the armament deal. But what if it is not about the countries themselves, but who stands to profit from the deal? What companies are providing the necessary equipment, materials, etc. needed to manufacture nuclear weapons? Blocking the deal would be very costly for any number of such companies. As it stands, the President is the biggest obstacle in getting it to go through."

"Dammit, Quint. I had not thought of that. Certainly, China, Iran, and Russia have denied any involvement in Dianna's kidnapping or the murder of Mrs. Northrup. North Korea's denial has been less vociferous, but it also has denied having anything to do with either event. I need you to start digging into the companies that were involved in the initial plans and those that hoped to get the winning bid to develop these weapons. That does not mean that they are being developed apart from the military complex of the individual countries, but someone must provide the necessary know-how and materials needed for actual production. In the meantime, Lila will continue working on these Russian characters. I am assigning Buster to chase down the guys that went after Sammy. I am going to give you a burner phone and a number where you can call Sammy and convince him that he can safely talk to Buster. Currently Sammy seems to think you are the only one that has his back."

Glancing at his watch, Gerald stood to signal the meeting was over. Quint arose as well, and the two men walked to the office door. Gerald clasped Quint on the shoulder, "Don't overdo it. I know you are safe in the White House, but I am assigning a security detail to cover you 24/7 until we get this figured out."

Quint groaned. Four days of being hovered over and monitored had left him thoroughly sick of the constant surveillance. He was accustomed to taking care of himself without babysitters assigned by his well-meaning friend.

Quint could not help the sharp note in his voice, "I know you mean well, but I can handle myself and far more discretely than I can with others tagging along."

"I'm your friend, Quint, but I'm also your boss. You will go along with this."

"Alright. But I don't like it."

Gerald chuckled. "I never thought you would. Now, let's go. I've got a White House dinner waiting and I'm running late. I suspect Lila is eager for you to get back too."

CHAPTER 16

The driver, Agent Morris, was waiting patiently in the non-descript black agency car when Quint walked out of the CIA offices and climbed into the back seat. Quint was tired, but strangely exhilarated to be out of the hospital and free to move around. The first thing he wanted to do when he reached the White House was find Lila, give her a kiss, and then take Code for a run prior to dinner.

Frequently the President invited them to join his daughter and him in the family quarters for a quiet meal. Dianna often engaged Lila in separate conversation while the two men talked. It was apparent to Quint that Lila was becoming a quasi-mother figure as Dianna sought advice and girl-talk in the absence of her mother. It was obvious the President was lonely, too. It was a dichotomy to be constantly surrounded by staff and guards, and yet experience a remoteness. The President seemed to seek simple human contact on a personal level free of the constraints that restricted those around him from over familiarity with the most powerful man on Earth. Losing his wife had only emphasized that loneliness. Nor had he yet come to grips with the cost to his family because of his political climb to the highest office in the land. Unlike many politicians, the man was inherently shy and slow to share thoughts beyond those related to his role. When Quint returned to his suite at the White House,

Lila was already there having stopped working for the day. She smiled when he entered.

After they had shared a hello kiss, she commented, "You would think after being in the hospital you would have come straight back here." Her chiding was mild but carried an undertone of concern.

"I'm sorry, babe. I am so frustrated from being out of the loop, I went straight to Gerald to share my theories about what is going on."

"I understand. Was he receptive to your ideas?"

"He gave me the go ahead, and to start digging into a new angle. Anything new in your search?"

"Nothing since the names that popped up. I am still looking into that."

"Do I have time to go for a walk with Code before dinner?"

"We have just over an hour before we are expected to join POTUS for dinner at 7:30. You need to get back in time to shower and change. I laid out your tux as he mentioned an ambassador joining us and maybe some others."

"Okay, thirty minutes with Code and I will come back and have a quick shower and change. That will give you the bathroom to yourself while we are out."

Lila shook her finger, "Don't you dare overdo it. The doctor said to take it easy for the next few days."

"I promise. Now, where is Code?"

"He is in the bathroom eating his dinner. Once he knows he is going for a walk with you, he is going to be one happy dog. He's been whining for you the entire time you were in the hospital as he sensed something was wrong. I swear that dog has more brains than some people."

"I agree. Maybe, we should run him for Congress." She was still laughing when he walked out to change into running clothes and fetch Code. The moment Quint walked into the bedroom Code came charging out of the bathroom barking with joy. In five minutes, they left the suite with a goodbye wave to Lila.

The early evening was cool with a light breeze. Quint smiled and waved as he trotted by the guards that peppered the grounds of the White House, ever vigilant for danger. The one that had followed him from the third floor, keeping a discrete distance, quietly swung in behind Quint. A happy tail-wagging Cord followed at Quint's heels. Quint would have loved to give the dog the good run they both so loved but remembering both the caution from Lila and the doctor to take it easy, he decided not to overdo it. He missed the carefree days roaming the sandy shore of Figure Eight with Cord and Lila. As soon as the current mystery was cleared and the President and his family were safe from the unknown threat, he intended to go home on the next plane headed to Wilmington. He looked toward the gate leading to the street but decided not to venture outside with night coming on. He had been attacked once. For all he knew, both Sammy and he had become ancillary threats.

At the appointed time Lila and Quint, dressed in evening attire, joined the other guests as they stood in the receiving line to greet the President and the Kazakhstan Ambassador, Jomart Vassilenko, in whose honor the dinner was being given. They stood in the doorway of the formal state dining room for a moment after they left the receiving line. Quint looked around the elegant room where they were to dine for the first time. Over one of the two fireplaces was a large portrait of Abraham Lincoln. Blue and cornsilk yellow striped drapes adorned the floor to ceiling windows. Although able to accommodate up to 120 people, Quint judged the round tables were set for approximately A gentle nudge on his elbow from Lila told him it was time to move to his assigned seat at the table furthest from the President and Ambassador Vassilenko. Lila's seat was across from him. Looking at the others as they stood awaiting the entry of the President and the Ambassador, the Vice President and Second Lady, Quint recognized several Senators, the Speaker of the House, Gerald Williams and his wife, a group of Ambassadors and their wives, senior White House staff including the Press Secretary, and four cabinet members. In the corner, the official military band awaited the playing of the national anthems of Kazakhstan and then the United States. On each of the round tables were the customary four wine glasses and ten pieces of flatware for the four-course meal. At that moment, Quint was grateful for the etiquette lessons his mother had insisted he take. He glanced across at Lila and noticed her unease as she too surveyed the elaborate table setting. He caught her eye and mouthed *just follow me*. A slight nod of her head indicated she understood.

A Kazakh chef had been arranged through the embassy to supplement traditional American fare with a main course of Kuurdak, a dish of braised beef and potatoes, and a fried honey cake dish for dessert called Chak-Chak. Both dishes were delicious as was the wine chosen for each course. Lila became more comfortable as the meal progressed and was enjoying her conversation with one of the Kazakh embassy staff who explained the dishes to her.

Quint was uncustomarily quiet during the meal as he watched an increasingly chilly interaction between the President and Vassilenko. He would have loved to be seated at the President's table to hear the conversation. It was apparent that the others at the table were uncomfortable at the direction things were going, particularly Gerald Williams who sat across from the President. He fully planned to discover what had led to the change in atmosphere between the two men by catching up with Gerald after the meal. Quint surmised that it was probably connected to the fact that Kazakhstan, a former Soviet Socialist Republic, was rich in minerals and reserves of gas and petroleum, particularly uranium needed by nuclear agencies around the world whether for fuel or weapons.

Director Williams confirmed Quint's suspicion when Quint corralled him as they left the State Dining room and stepped apart from the others in the hall. According to him, the President had questioned to whom Kazakhstan was selling uranium. The Ambassador had immediately stiffened and avoided answering despite President Northrup repeating the question. After that, communication between the two was decidedly sparse. Gerald Williams and Quint both realized that the President was convinced that it was a cabal of four rogue nations behind the recent attacks on him and his family…and now he would suspect Kazakhstan as well.

When Quint and Lila returned to their suite, he immediately logged on to his laptop and started searching information on Kazakhstan. The largest landlocked country in the world had been rocked several times over the years by various scandals, some connected to US officials who had enriched themselves through double dealing. The mostly Muslim country was formed on December 16, 1991, when it broke away from the former Soviet Union and declared its independence. As second richest in the world in reserves of lead, chromium, zinc, and uranium and eleventh richest in gas and petroleum, the country enjoyed robust trade giving the population of over nineteen million a relatively good economy despite an authoritarian rule. Of particular interest to Quint was the list of companies dealing in uranium, so vital to the production of nuclear energy and warheads. He began making a list of the companies he would have the CIA research:

1. *Kazatompron, 21% of Kazahk uranium exports.*
2. *Cameco, with offices in Canada, 15%.*
3. *Orano with offices in Saskatchewan, Niger, and Kazakhstan, 13%.*
4. *Uranium One, Russian state owned with offices in Canada, the US, Tanzania, Kazakhstan, and selling to nuclear utilities in Russia, Europe, North America, the Middle East, and Asia, 5%.*
5. *National Nuclear Corp and China General Nuclear Power, Chinese, 4%.*
6. *ARMZ a Russian owned holding company operated by Atomenergoprom, 5%.*
7. *AtomKaz, unknown ownership due to various holding companies and investment partnerships, % unknown.*

After Quint had compiled the list, he leaned back and began to study the companies he had listed. If the threats were the result of the nuclear deal that the countries of North Korea, China, Russia, and Iran wanted to pursue, then he would look more closely at 4, 5, and 6. However, if it were not the countries, but a business aggressively pursuing the deal, which of them was the most likely candidate? Kazatompron represented 21% of the world's supply of uranium and potentially would have the most to lose if a large deal went sour. AtomKaz was probably operating in some fashion from Kazakhstan judging from the second part of the name, however what amount they produced and how important a sales deal would be to them was an unknown factor. That made four of the companies with ties to Kazakhstan. If the Russian holding company ARMZ was included, the number came to five. With that kind of economic interest in any nuclear deal between the four countries, it might well explain the chilly climate between Ambassador Vassilenko and the President.

Lila wandered in from the bedroom rubbing sleep from her eyes. He felt guilty that he had all but ignored her from the moment they had returned to their suite. He gave her a smile full of contrition. "I'm sorry if I'm keeping you up, but I have a real hunch I'm trying to get a handle on."

She could not keep the exasperation from her voice, "It's three in the morning. I really think your hunch could wait a few more hours."

Quint shut down his computer and stood up. Taking her by the hand he led her back to the bedroom. By the time he undressed, brushed his teeth, and crawled into bed beside her, she was fast asleep. He suspected sleep would prove more elusive for him. Not knowing the source of the threats, he knew there was not a moment to spare.

The sound of footsteps thundering down the hall roused Quint from restless slumber. Lifting up he looked at the bedside clock…3:45. He did not have time to process what was going on before there was a hammering on the door of their suite. Jumping out of bed, he glanced over at Lila who had sat up. "I'll see what it is. Try to go back to sleep."

"Fat chance!"

"Hang on while I see what they want."

Quint donned his robe, tying the sash as he walked to the door. Two security guards along beside the one assigned to him stood there panting. He demanded, "What's going on?"

"We don't know but there has been a disruption to our security cameras shortly after an alarm sounded. The President and his daughter are already in the bunker. You need to join the staff and go to the bunker, too, until we can ascertain the cause and secure the building."

"Take my wife. I'm going to join you guys and do what I can to help."

The man's eyes narrowed as he looked Quint directly in the eye, "No can do. My orders are to evacuate everyone to the bunker immediately. I'm not going against direct orders."

Quint studied the guard for a minute, before growling, "So be it. I'll get my wife."

Lila spoke up from behind him, "I'm ready. Let's go."

Quint and Lila joined a stream of White House staff headed below. All were half awake but scurrying like ants from a kicked over ant hill. Frustrated by the President's order to join the others in the bunker, Quint decided to disobey. He would deal with the fallout later. He began to lag behind Lila until others formed a wall between them. When he was in the rear of the hustling crowd, he quietly peeled away into a side corridor. He ignored Lila's voice calling to him from further down the main hallway. She would be furious. However, he was determined to not only find the responsible parties for the recent attacks, but to stop them for good. After the group had passed down the hall and vanished from view, Quint ducked out. He had not gone ten paces before the security guard assigned to him hollered at him to stop. Quint turned and waited as Special Agent Murphy approached him. Quint did not wait for him to begin, but cut him off by saying, "I'm going to join these guys like it or not, your orders or not. I have a special assignment from both the CIA and the President to find out who is behind the attacks on the President and his family and stop them. My wife and I are staying in the White House at the specific request of the President to deal with just this kind of incident. He personally gave me leeway to do whatever I deem necessary. If the Director of the CIA or anyone else gives you any flack, tell them I directly disobeyed you. I'll deal with it. Now, tell me what you know."

"Hell, I don't know a damned thing other than the alarm signaling an intrusion went off and all our cameras went blank. The protocol is immediate evacuation to the Bunker."

"Have you tried to communicate with the roof top guards and those around the perimeter of the grounds?"

"I can't. That has been blocked, too."

Quint swore under his breath. "What is the protocol once everyone is secure in the bunker?"

"We sweep the building checking all entry points. Others are already checking the main floor which is the first step."

"What was the location of the initial alarm?"

"That's the weird thing. It was the roof. How that happened, I don't have a clue."

"So why start from the bottom up? The problem may well be on the upper floor where the President resides."

The guard gnawed on his lip for a moment before replying. "I see what you mean."

Quint jerked his thumb towards the stairs that led up. "Screw protocol. I'm going up there. I could use your help."

Murphy's Adam's apple bobbed as he swallowed hard. "Okay, okay. I don't like this, but I'm with you. It's my job to keep you safe, but you aren't making it easy. I'll snag a couple of others to go with us."

"Okay, let's roll."

CHAPTER 17

Quint, Murphy, and the two others skidded to a stop when they stepped out onto the roof. The guards that had been securing the area were sprawled in every direction. With blood seeping under their shoes, Quint and the other three men began the gruesome task to see if any still lived. Judging by the wounds they had been shot from above by a high caliber gun or guns. Forensics would determine the angle and the bullets used. The puzzle was how they could have been shot from above? Why did the guards not realize the danger and have time to react? And, most troubling of all, where were the killer or killers now? Of the six downed men, only one had a faint pulse. Agent Murphy snatched his phone from his pocket and called for an ambulance. Quint knelt down and pressed on the wound in the man's chest. Slowly the man's eyes fluttered open.

"Take it easy. We're calling for an ambulance to treat you. Can you tell us what happened?"

His voice barely a whisper, the man said, "Drones shot us. Must have had silencers as we didn't hear them firing rounds. After we had been shot, three men with personal propulsion jets landed on the roof. They went to the command room up here and cut the feed to the videos. I played dead and…" With his voice fading away, he closed his eyes.

Quint called one of the agents over, "Stay with this man and keep pressure on his wound. I'm going to look for the bastards that did this." He left two agents to deal with the lone survivor and the bodies of the other five men and signaled Murphy to follow him. Leaving the roof, he spotted the jet packs lying on the corner of the roof. He signaled to Murphy to help him disable them so the attackers could not use them to escape.

While they were working, Quint asked Murphy if he knew anything about the Jet Packs. Murphy nodded his head, "I'm fascinated by the things. These are called the "Daedalus" named for the guy in mythology that flew too close to the sun and melted the wax in his wings. They were designed by Richard Browning and made by his company, Gravity Industries in Salisbury, England. Hell, you can buy them at that department store…what's it called?…oh, yeah…Selfridges in London. That's provided you have close to a half million per. Currently he has the only viable ones on the market. On my salary I won't be buying one unless I win the lottery. By the way, various branches of our own military have a few of them."

Quint snatched the wires and gas feeds from the last Daedalus as Murphy indicated he had finished with the one he was working on. "I hope we can rule out that these were from our guys. Let's find these evil SOBs before they can kill anyone else." After they descended to the third floor, Quint and Murphy began a fast but thorough check of every room and closet. In his own suite Quint found Code frantically clawing at the bathroom door where they had left him. Quint stopped long enough to quickly soothe his dog and don the clothes he had discarded before going to bed. He did not intend to resume the search wearing his pajamas. When they finished scouring the third floor, they began a search of the second floor where the President's rooms were located. The second floor was also empty of any occupants and contained no signs of the invaders. On the first floor, the doors were secured with guards standing on the exterior to keep any other intruders from entering. Judging from the bullet holes in the wall near the exit to the basement, and a trickle of blood on the floor there, someone had been shot. Glancing over his shoulder, Quint saw exterior guards had entered the foyer and were granting admittance to three EMT's who were wheeling in a gurney.

He walked over to the men, and said, "You'll find a wounded agent on the roof. He's badly hurt."

"Where's the roof access?"

Before Quint could answer, the two guards he had left on the roof ran up. The first one, Nobles, shook his head; panting he gasped, "The poor guy didn't make it. The only thing up there now is six bodies."

"Damn," Quint swore and turned back to the medics. "You guys go back out and stay low. There may be more injured downstairs. We won't know until we get down there. If we need you, we will call the security guards out front to send you back in when it's safe."

Quint asked in an urgent voice barely above a whisper, "Can you guys get me into the tunnel that leads from here to the PEOC under the East Wing?"

Murphy replied, "That we can. It's a part of our training when we graduate to the senior level to get access to the Presidential Emergency Operations Center. Come on."

Murphy walked at a rapid pace from the main hall with Quint and the other two agents dogging his heels. Murphy led the way through an inconspicuous door hidden in the wall and down a flight of steps to a tunnel. To gain access Murphy had to first go through both digital and retinal biometric scans. Once in the tunnel, they rushed to the door of the elevator. Lying on the floor were four agents. Quint noted one was missing both his right index finger and an eyeball. He swore under his breath. He met Murphy's eyes which had filled with tears.

"He was a friend of yours?"

"Yeah. Since I was a kid. Chris is the one that got me this job."

"That's tough." Quint put his hand on Murphy's shoulder, "Can we take a stairway down the five stories to the bunker? I don't feel much like taking the elevator not knowing what might be waiting when it stops."

Murphy nodded and walked towards a door leading to a stairway. Giving him time to collect himself, Agents Coggins and Nobles led the way to give Murphy time to refocus. When they reached the fifth level down, they could hear gunfire. Swearing, Coggins cracked open the door to see what was happening. Since the invaders were using silencers, he assumed the louder gunfire was coming from the White House Security guards. After a moment, he pulled his head back in and softly closed the door.

Whispering, he informed the others, "Two of the perps are hiding behind supports on each side of the hall and returning fire from our guys, the other one is lying on the floor bleeding. I can't tell how badly hurt he is, but he's out of action. The invaders are between us and our agents. We can flank them and take them out without much trouble. The main thing is to avoid being shot by friendly fire."

Quint nodded, "How far down the hall are they from us?"

"Maybe forty feet."

"Are there any support walls between here and them that we can take cover behind?"

"Yes. Ten or twelve feet down."

His adrenaline pumping, Quint nodded, "Okay, we will take our shoes off as a precaution. With the shooting we probably wouldn't be heard, but I'm not taking chances. Murphy and I will take the left side. You two take the other."

The three agents nodded. Easing the door open the four men split into twos and sprinted to the defilade points Coggins had indicated. From his station, Quint drew a bead on the guy on the right side. At the same time, Nobles aimed at the one on the left. When both men were ready, Coggins signaled them to fire at the same time. Both invaders fell to the floor bleeding from multiple wounds. They would be dead in seconds. The agents that were defending the entrance to the bunker emerged and checked the bodies.

Quint called, "Are they dead?"

"Yeah. Do you know if there are any more of these bad guys in here?"

Coggins answered, "There doesn't appear to be. Do you have any injured men?"

"Yeah, three around the corner. Two of them were seriously hit. One is dead. One of our guys is applying tourniquets and doing what he can until EMT gets here."

"I'll get help." Coggins pulled out his phone and called the external security to have them send down the EMT guys.

The other three walked up to where the guards stood surrounding the two invader's bodies while Quint walked over to the first invader that had been shot. Kneeling beside him, he checked for a pulse. "Hey, we need to get this one to the hospital fast. I need him alive for interrogation."

Coggins walked over to Quint, "What can I do to help?"

"How about applying pressure to slow down the bleeding. I want to check the elevator to see if any of our guys are in there and need help. Someone will have to grant me access."

Nobles walked up, "I'll take care of that."

"Thanks." Quint dug his phone from his pocket and speed dialed Gerald to let him know what was happening.

After listening to Quint for several minutes, Gerald swore before adding, "I'm sending a security team to the hospital to cover the intruder and make sure nothing happens to him. Have White House security keep the President in the bunker until I get back to you. I plan to mess with some minds."

"Will do."

Gerald continued, "Yeah, I want whoever is behind this to think the invaders have the President locked down, and they are controlling access to the bunker. This should also keep them from learning that we have a survivor and take him out before he can talk. This is going to be one tricky press release while we ensure the guy survives and can talk. I intend to keep any information on the actual status of the invasion quiet until we can figure out how to go forward. I will inform the President I am creating a fictitious scenario whereby the Vice President is assuming command until we are free to announce the actual status. He's going to be mad as hell to be kept locked up, but that seems like the smartest move we have. I will have the Vice President address the nation that the President is being held hostage in the bunker and he is assuming command. I also intend to assure the Veep that this is an intelligence ploy to discover who is behind the ongoing attacks and he is not acting for the President who will continue in command."

"What else do you want us to do here?"

"Lock that place down so tight a flea can't get in...both inside and out. Once you relay that message, leave it to the security detail. You and Murphy meet me at the hospital. We're going to get this SOB to talk one way or another."

By the time Quint had finished his conversation with Gerald, the EMT guys were wheeling in gurneys, and Nobles stated he had found only blood stains in the elevator. They would be tested to identify the source when forensics did a sweep of the area. Quint hurriedly summoned Coggins to join Nobles. He instructed them as to what the CIA director was planning and his expectations of them. He left them to follow through on Gerald Williams directions to shut things down by assigning the security detail to all the various points needed to lock down both building and grounds.

"By the way, do not open the bunker and let folks out until either I or the Director get back to you with an all clear. Director Williams is going to call the President and inform him what he is planning." Quint turned to Murphy who was hovering nearby. "You are still attached to my ass, so come on. We are riding in the ambulance with the bad guy. If he even comes to a little bit, I intend to find out who in the hell planned this damned assault." Once the EMT guys had loaded the wounded invader on the gurney, Quint and his ever-present bodyguard Murphy followed them up in the elevator. Quint's brain was in overdrive. If he could tie the invaders to one of the companies in Kazakhstan, he could go after the perpetrators and shut them down. With the plot a result of commercial rather than national concerns, unless a country was also involved, much international pressure between nations would be resolved. This could well be his best chance of proving his theory, and he did not intend to blow it.

Despite protest from the EMT team, Quint seated himself beside the badly injured perp while Murphy sat up front in the passenger seat. The radio was on. They had just pulled out of the White House grounds, when the voice of the Vice President came on. The CIA Director had wasted no time putting his plan into action. Quint listened as the Veep described an on-going situation in the White House and that he was assuming emergency control of the nation. The main thing at this point was to keep the person or persons behind the invasion unaware that it had failed and that one of the invaders was captured and hopefully would be able to talk...willingly or otherwise.

With the siren blaring, the ambulance headed to the hospital. Despite the hostile stare of the EMT guy, Quint did a methodical search of the injured man's pockets. Flipping open the wallet, he found only a few bills and no identification of any kind. He wrapped the wallet in his handkerchief and slipped it into his own pocket. Forensics would go through the wallet with a fine-toothed comb. The EMT glared and started to say something but was stopped by Quint's upheld hand. He was in no mood for objections as he hovered over the injured man willing him to come to. When the ambulance came to a screeching halt at the emergency room entrance, a disappointed Quint, trailed by Murphy, followed the gurney taking the man into treatment. Now they would have to get around doctors before they could talk to the perp.

Inside the door of the emergency room, an anxious CIA director was pacing the floor. His head snapped up the minute the automated doors slid open. Spotting Quint, he hurried over.

Quint stalled his questions by shrugging his shoulders and shaking his head. Gerald Williams scowled as he approached the gurney and looked down at the man that had dared to attack his President. "I suppose the bastard is still out of it."

Quint's comment was bitter, "Yeah. If he comes around, the docs are going to treat us like pariahs unless you put the fear of God into them. One way or another, if this man gains consciousness, we are going to have to make him talk. If he's dying, we won't have much time. If he survives, maybe we can use him to put a further snag into things."

"Precisely what I'm thinking. By the way, did you go through his pockets?"

"Absolutely. I have his wallet. The wallet is not going to be much help as it only contained some money, no ID. About all we can get from it is where it was made and his fingerprints."

Quint turned the wallet over to the Director. "Thanks, Quint. Good move. My agents will get to work on this as soon as we can get it to Langley. Where it was made could prove useful, too, even without an ID. I suppose an ID was too much to hope for."

"White House security is searching the other two perps' bodies to see if they can learn anything from them."

CHAPTER 18

The minute the perp was being wheeled into surgery from the intake area, Gerald Williams flashed his credentials at the orderly. "Before you do another damned thing, understand that I am going with you to talk to the surgeon. This man just tried to kill our President. I hope you realize the gravity of that?"

The orderly, whose eyes resembled saucers, stuttered, "Ye... yes, sir."

"Good. Now, move on. Quint you come with me. Murphy, wait here. As soon as we arrange things with the doctor we'll be back. In the meantime, I have a security detail arriving shortly. Hang with them until we know where this asshole is going after surgery...assuming he survives."

Murphy nodded and stepped back. Gerald and Quint followed as the injured man was wheeled through the double doors. Quint suspected if the doctor gave any static, he was going to have his ass handed to him. The CIA director was spitting mad. He supposed part of the Director's anger was because the people that invaded the White House had bypassed all existing security measures. There was going to be a come-to- Jesus-moment when the Director got back to his office and reviewed security protocol.

In the meantime, Murphy figured he would make himself comfortable. Seated in the waiting area, he watched as his fellow agents were wheeled in for treatment. He prayed they would be luckier than his friend who had been mutilated by the invaders. He just hoped the Chris was dead when they gouged out his eye and cut off his finger. Murphy shut his eyes and willed the image of his friend from his mind. He just couldn't deal with it. He did not know if he ever would erase the scene from his memory. He knew when he joined the Agency there would be challenges and danger. The reality was all too near.

Beyond the closed doors, Gerald Williams walked up to the waiting surgeon. After showing his credentials to the surgeon, he wasted no words in specifying what he expected. "This man just invaded the White House and tried to kill the President. My agents are being wheeled in now for treatment. Some of them may die. I am in no mood for any static from anyone, so heed my words. If you can get this man to wake up before you anesthetize him for surgery, I am going to question him. If not, and he survives surgery, the first face he's going to see when he comes to is mine. You are going to see that happens. Do you understand?"

"I'm sorry about your men. I am trusting my colleagues to see to it they get the best care we can offer. You must realize that my priority is to my patient regardless of what he may or may not have done. That means, I am the final authority on whether the patient is stable enough to respond to any interrogation."

"To hell with your authority. In this case, I am the one that has final say. Like it or not, I am going into that room with you while you make an initial assessment of his condition. I want to know if he is shaming unconsciousness, or if it is for real. I want to know what his chances of survival are. When I can determine that with your assistance, I will leave you to it. If prior to surgery, he is capable of responding to questions, I damned well intend to ask them. I am sorry if that sticks in your craw, but that's how it's going to be."

"Christ, what a mess." The doctor cursed under his breath before growling, "Since you insist, come with me. Once we go into surgery, you are out. Until then, if he can talk, I won't stop you."

"Let's go." Gerald's voice was grimly determined as he met the doctor's eyes.

Grudgingly the doctor nodded.

Quint and Gerald walked behind the gurney as the patient was wheeled into the pre-surgery area. While the doctor was focused ahead, Quint winked at Gerald who raised an eyebrow in question. Quint merely smiled as he reached over and punched the perp in his groin. The man gasped and his eyes blinked open as his hands cupped himself.

The doctor looked over his shoulder at the man's gasp, "What's going on?"

Gerald commented, "He appears to be aware after all, doctor. Why don't you go scrub up while we see what we can learn." When the doctor seemed to hesitate, Gerald barked, "That was an order, not a request."

Grumbling under his breath, the doctor left. The moment the surgery door closed, Gerald leaned over the man and barked, "Who are you and who sent you?"

The man stared up at him with incomprehension. He groaned before muttering in Russian.

"Dammit," Gerald swore. "I don't think he speaks English."

"That was Russian. I'm no whiz at it, but I speak some. Let me see what I can get out of him."

"Go for it."

With halting Russian, Quint began the interrogation. "What is your name and for whom are you working? If you don't answer and give us what we need you are going to die right here. We are going to hurt you a lot worse than you are now before we let you die if you lie to us. So, make sure you answer correctly." Quint's Russian was heavily accented, but the guy looked at him with fear in his eyes.

The perp whispered, "I'm Vassily Morosov. Please help me."

Gerald looked at Quint and nodded. This was the second man that they were looking for in connection with Dianna's abduction. Quint glowered at him, "We've been looking for you. Now, tell us where you're from and who you work for."

"Kazakhstan."

"Are you working for your government."

The man's voice was barely audible when he answered, "No. So much pain, help me." Vassily groaned and closed his eyes.

Quint shook him roughly, "Hey wake up. Who hired you?"

Vassily opened his mouth to speak but only managed to croak, "Ato..." With that he lapsed into unconsciousness.

Gerald looked at the man and swore. "So, what did you learn? All I caught was his name and Kazakhstan."

"He's not working for the government of Kazakhstan which is good news. He started to tell me the name of who he's working for but all he got out was 'Ato...'."

"Does that mean anything to you?"

"If it is a company doing business in Kazakhstan, there are two that begin with an 'Ato.' One is a Russian owned uranium holding company called Atomenerzoprom operating as ARMZ. The other is AtomKaz. I could find nothing to tell me who the owners are. The second one appears to be a shell holding company that is deliberately obscure as to direct ownership."

"So, is this character Russian?"

"He says he's from Kazakhstan."

"I suppose that doesn't tell us if he's connected to Russia since the official language of the country is Russian as Kazakhstan was once part of the USSR."

"Right, they got their independence in December of '91."

"Then possibly either the Russians or a Kazakhstan company with ties to Russia is behind this."

"It could also be one of the other countries that does business with either of the two companies I named. With AtomKaz, we're in the dark since I don't yet know the owners. Numerous countries buy uranium from Kazakhstan. It could be any number of bad actors whether corporate or government. My hunch is it's corporate."

"Put Lila on this AtomKaz and see what she can learn. I may need to send you and Buster over there to do some snooping. What does he speak besides Chinese?"

Quint and Buster, a former SEAL and contract operative for the CIA, had worked on numerous cases, and they were comfortable with one another despite Buster's deliberate flirting with Lila in an attempt to tease Quint. Quint had accepted it was harmless on Buster's part. The perennial bachelor, having never learned to settle down, could not resist flirting with anything in skirts. Despite the teasing, the two men liked one another and there was no one that Quint would rather have in his corner when things got tough.

Quint thought for a moment before responding, "If I remember correctly, he speaks Mandarin, plus: German, Spanish,

Italian, and I think Vietnamese. I speak French, Italian, and some Russian. But my accent in Russian is lousy."

"If we find out that North Korea is in on this, I'm going to call in Donald Compton. He speaks Korean well. You remember him?"

"Yes, of course. He's the one that did the interrogation of Pah Pong Ju when he fled North Korea."

"Yeah, Pah's under witness protection in a safe house with a new name."

"Is he worth using for his language ability?"

"I'd rather have Compton. He is a shrewd operative and one of the best I have in Asia. Pah doesn't have the chops to be of any use with this. Besides, he is too tense most of the time. He's convinced the North Koreans are going to put a hit out on him for defecting. I can't say I blame him. Despite every precaution, sometimes things screw up. We both know those bastards won't stop until Pah's dead."

A nurse appeared at the door of the surgery interrupting their discussion. "The doctor says you are finished here for now. I am here to take the patient into surgery. Give me your phone number, and he will call as soon as this man is out of surgery and can talk."

Gerald handed over his business card. "Mr. Cord will be waiting here the minute he is lucid." He grumbled, "Remind the doctor what I said."

When the nurse looked down at the card, her eyebrows climbed her forehead. She gulped, "Yes, sir. Director Williams."

Quint and Gerald watched as the unconscious Vassily Morosov was wheeled into surgery. Gerald asked Quint to stay behind to be available the moment the man was out of surgery and conscious. Quint nodded in agreement and retreated to the waiting room to grab a chair while Gerald left to check on the injured agents. Settling himself into a seat with a direct view of the surgery door, Quint shook his head with disgust at the recent frequency of sitting in waiting rooms. With time on his hands, he called Lila to fill her in on what was happening and to ask her to dig into the AtomKaz company ownership and customers. With her expertise, if information could be had, she would find it. Next he called Buster to clue him in on what was happening and the possibility of a trip to Kazakhstan in the near future.

"Kazakhstan! I have absolutely no interest in going there. I've been. I don't like the food, don't speak the language, and don't like the women. Speaking of women, last night I met a smoking hot little thing. It's too soon for me to head off to parts unknown as she is a real looker, and I'm sure not the only one chasing her."

Quint snorted, "I don't think Gerald is going to be interested in the details of your bird-dogging. At any rate, it's not a sure thing; I'm just giving you a heads up. Just chill, brother, and think about the cash you will earn. It sounds like you are going to need it to entertain your new girl-toy."

"Look, smart ass. She's different. I think this might be the one."

"Yeah, yeah. I've heard that before at least a dozen times." Quint snorted.

"Yeah, yeah." Peeved, Buster mocked Quint. He abruptly ended the conversation with, "Call me when you know something definite. I've got better things to do besides jaw on the phone."

"That went well," Quint muttered to himself. With Buster off the phone, he leaned his head back against the wall and closed his eyes. Due to the invasion of the White House, his sleep had been cut short and he felt spent. There was no way of knowing how long surgery would take, and then recovery, before the man would be out from under sedation. Within minutes he had nodded off. He did not know how long he slept. Quint jerked awake with a start. Standing up, he stretched and paced back and forth across the waiting lounge. Looking around he noted he was not the only one bored with the wait. Some were sleeping; others kept glancing anxiously at the board showing patient numbers and status. He had not noticed the electronic display board before, nor had he been given a patient number, so he could only wait not knowing what was happening with the perp. Needing some caffeine to make him more alert, he walked over to the Keurig station, selected a dark roast coffee, double strength, and waited for it to brew. That done, he returned to his seat and sipped on the steaming cup.

As he sipped, he studied the austere waiting room and those who like him awaited news of someone in surgery. Some were reading books on their iPads or paperbacks that they had fished out of a canvas bag on the seat beside them. Others were scrolling through their phones. He guessed they were answering emails or posting on Facebook. One or two were staring with glazed over eyes at the muted television seeming lost in numb misery. Some sat anxiously watching the electronic display board where they tracked the slow progress of whomever they were praying for as they awaited the doctor's prognosis. A few sat in quiet contemplation or prayer, eyes closed, hands clasped tightly in their laps. Quint could not help being reminded of his own angst as he waited for Lila to come out of a coma following an auto accident.

He looked up as the door to surgery swung open, and the doctor walked toward him. Quint could read in his face that things had not gone well. Raising his brows in question, Quint stood.

The doctor led him to a conference room and shut the door. Quint watched him as he grimaced and shook his head. "I did what I could, but it wasn't enough. Do you have a name and address, next of kin, etc. I can put on the death certificate?"

Quint swore under his breath before nodding. "His name is Vassily Morozov. He said he is from Kazakhstan. We will need to check with immigration control and the Kazakh embassy to see if any other details are available. Someone from the CIA will get back to you with any further information and instructions for the disposition of the body."

"Right. I'm sorry I couldn't do more as I realize he may have been of some help to you in learning who is behind the attacks on the President. The man had too much internal damage. No matter how hard we try, there are some we cannot save."

"Thank you for trying. I hope you understand we had no option but to hard-nose you."

"Under the circumstances, I suppose I can understand why Director Williams gave his orders, but I damned well don't like it as my priority is the welfare of my patients."

"Look, we get it. But when it's a matter of critical National importance, other things take precedence. If we had not interrogated him before surgery, we would not know his name. If it makes you feel any better, he's one of the men that abducted the President's daughter and murdered her classmate."

After the doctor left without making a comment, Quint called Gerald with the bad news. "Thanks, Quint. On a more positive note, it looks as though our agents will pull through."

"Thank God for that."

CHAPTER 19

When Quint returned from the hospital, Lila glanced up from her computer in their suite before continuing to type commands. Knowing better than to interrupt, Quint gave her a kiss on the forehead before heading for the shower. He hoped it would revive him enough to function despite losing most of the previous night's sleep. He peeled off his clothes and dropped them to the bathroom floor as he waited for the water to get hot. Reaching in, he tested it with his fingers. Flinching at the heat, Quint lowered the water to a tolerable temperature. Stepping in, he let the water beat on him until he could feel some of the stress and weariness draining from his bones. He wondered how Lila could be so focused as she had not had any more sleep than he had. No way were the White House evacuees settled into comfortable beds when they were hustled into the secure bunker. Quint finished his shower and toweled dry before donning a fresh set of clothes. He had work to do if they were going to stop the on-going assaults against the President.

He went back into the sitting room where Lila was yawning as she typed away. He shook his head as he walked up to her. "Hey, babe. Go take a shower. It will help to wake you up."

Without looking up, she continued typing as she mumbled, "Not right now. I think I'm on to something." Quint had turned to leave when she shouted, "I've got it! I. Have. Got. It."

"What?"

"It took some tracking, but I discovered the ownership of the AtomKaz corporation. It is the Medvev Group. I typed in 'medvev' and learned that means "bear' in Russian and Kazak. I guess I've tracked the bear!"

"What else have you learned about them?"

Lila grinned as she turned from the computer screen. "The corporate website says it is owned by unnamed Russian and Kazakh partners who are trading in uranium to North Korea, and Iran in particular. The President's interest in shutting down nuclear weapons in those countries could have triggered them to come against him as they are Medvev's primary customers."

"I'll call Gerald and let him know what you've learned. He will want you to text him everything you know. I need a printout of any names of the partners and anything you can find on them, as well. In the meantime, once you know the names, I suspect he's going to want you to do some digging into their associates, and their whereabouts."

"That was my next step." Lila pushed herself from the chair. "However, at the moment I'm beat to a frazzle. I think I will have that shower before I start digging." She turned back on the way to the bathroom to add, "Dianna sat with me in the bunker. She was terrified and kept crying. I think she needs to get away from here for a while. Do you think Gerald would allow me to work from home on Figure Eight? With a safe room in our house, and Dianna's security detail, we should be fine. I think the beach and some time walking along the shore with Code would get her mind off the kidnapping, her mother's death, and now the attack here at the White House. Besides, Teresa would love the chance to coddle her with tempting goodies. I could use coddling myself."

"Damn, I would miss you and Code, but I see the sense of it. Dianna's had more to deal with than any teenager should. It is hard enough living in the White House and constantly in the public eye, dealing with the angst of growing up, and now the constant danger. I will talk with Gerald first, and if he gives me the go-ahead, maybe we could sit down with the President and tell him what we propose. He's not going to be happy to have her out of his eyesight, but I think he will see it might be best for her to get away for a few days."

"Thanks, Quint. I don't want to leave you either, but it breaks my heart that she has endured so much. Tell Gerald I'll get those names and any info to him before we go. Once I've done that, the rest will be up to him to decide how to deal with it."

Walking to Lila, Quint pulled her into his arms. "You have a good heart, Lila. I love you more than you know. When this is over, I promise to give you all the coddling you can stand. I am sorry I don't have time to do it right now."

"Umm...I could use some special attention, but I'll wait. I love you, too. Now, I'm going for that shower while you get back to business."

"I'm off. I'll see you after I meet with Gerald."

"Let's talk to the President prior to dinner...before Dianna comes in. I wouldn't want to get her hopes up only to be dashed."

"I'll run it by Gerald and if he's good with it, I'll set up a meeting with the President before we go to dinner."

"Great...now to the shower for me."

Quint left the suite to find his shadow waiting in the hallway. "Hey, Murphy. I'm going to headquarters to meet with the Director. I guess you are supposed to drive me?"

"Those are my orders. I'm supposed to stick to you like Velcro. Otherwise, Director Williams will have my ass."

"Mine, too, if I don't go along with it. I don't see me as a target, but he damned sure does."

"Better safe than sorry."

Quint added, "By the way, in North Carolina some say cocklebur instead of Velcro. If you have ever walked through a patch of them, you know how they stick."

Quint and Murphy spent nearly an hour navigating snarled traffic to reach Langley. Sitting beside Murphy in the front seat, Quint closed his eyes and napped until they pulled in at the security gate. While not entirely rested, he felt a little better. Murphy had phoned ahead to alert the Director they were on the way. When they reached his office, Quint was immediately ushered in. Gerald was sitting at his desk, a pile of broken pencils in front of him. Quint chuckled to himself as he wondered how many government-issued pencils Gerald had broken over the years. Somehow, it had become the man's safety valve when he was frustrated.

Quint nodded at the pencils littering the desk, "Bad day?"

"Hell. That is the understatement of the year. I have dead and injured agents, an attempt on the President's life, an invasion of the White House which was supposed to be safe from any such attempts, Morosov who could have answered questions is in the morgue, the hospital administrator chewed my ass for coercing his doctor…Yeah, you could say it's a bad day. If you have anything else that will make it worse, we're having a shot of bourbon before we even start on why you're here."

"Nah, I think I can offer a little hope, but I'll have that bourbon anyway. I could also use a big juicy cheeseburger from the café while we talk. I am about starved."

"I'll have a couple sent up…medium, all the way?"

"Medium, ketchup, mustard, onion, tomato, and lettuce. And extra crispy fries. While you order our lunch, I'll pour that bourbon."

With the order phoned down to the café, and the bourbon poured, Gerald leaned back in his desk and said, "Okay, now try to make my day better."

Quint took a sip of the Woodford bourbon before replying, "Lila hacked into AtomKaz and did some poking around. The company is owned entirely by the Russian-Kahzakh holding company Medvev. She says Medvev means 'bear' in Russian and she's digging now to find the principals in the company."

"So, our question becomes did our Russian bear leave enough tracks for us to tie these attacks to Medvev?"

"Right." Quint paused, "There's another issue we need to address. Dianna Northrup is close to a meltdown. Lila has spent enough time with the girl to know that this latest attack has her teetering on the breaking point. Lila suggested she take Dianna to our house on Figure Eight. With the fortified saferoom, it's secure.„not as much as here, but safe. Plus, they will have Dianna's security detail with them. If you think it's workable, we will run it by the President before we say anything to Dianna."

Gerald bowed his head and clasped his hands in front of his forehead for a couple of minutes. Quint waited for him to think it through. With kids of his own, the Director was more than aware of the pressures on families in high positions. Blowing out his breath, Gerald raised his head. "God help her, Dianna must be tough not to have broken before now. I'll assign a couple of extra assets from our Wilmington office to augment the regular security detail. Whether she's on Figure Eight or at the White House, I still need Lila to keep digging."

"Don't worry. When she sinks her teeth into something, she's like a jealous bulldog with a bone. She's not going to let go until she's gnawed off all the meat."

"Once she gives us the names behind Medvev, you and Buster are going to see to it they cause no more trouble…no matter what it takes, or who they are." Gerald Williams' eyes were like steel when he said it. He did not need to define the assignment. Some things were better left unarticulated.

A knock on the door announced the arrival of their lunch. Without being asked, Quint refreshed their drinks and joined the Director at the table in front of the brown leather sofa that occupied the far wall of the office. The custom sofa had been especially ordered to provide the length and comfort needed to accommodate the Director when he was forced to sleep in the office. Both men seated themselves on opposite ends of the sofa and dug into their lunch with relish. Neither did any talking as they were too busy eating, but their brains did not stop churning. When they had finished and sipped the last of their bourbon, Gerald returned to his seat behind his desk and Quint took the one in front of it.

Gerald returned to their earlier conversation. "I can talk to the President about Dianna, but I think it would be better coming from Lila. I will assure him Lila can continue working from Figure Eight and we can keep them safe there. I might even consider sending the President with them for an unannounced vacation until I can work out a new security protocol for the White House. Is that feasible? I know you have the needed technology to keep him up to speed on communications, etc."

"As you know the only way onto the island is through a bridge checkpoint manned by island security. That leaves it up to us to arrange air and sea patrol to be added to the security level. It would be a good idea to contact the Figure Eight management company and advise them that you will be supplementing the bridge security with assets from our Wilmington office. If no one knows the President's location, it will be safer for all concerned, but we still need to cover all the bases."

"Absolutely. The more I think about it the better I like the idea of getting them both out of Washington until we can compromise the culprits behind these attacks. If you have no objections, I'll be inviting myself to that before dinner meeting with President Northrup, Lila, and you."

"I like it. Getting away from the fishbowl will also give Dianna and her dad a chance to spend some needed time together without the pressures they face here. Now we have two things to convince him of. Frankly, I think he will be happier to be with her than for them to be separated."

"I suspect you're right." Gerald paused, "I'm going to arrange for a meeting with the President before he goes in to dinner. Clue Lila in on what's up as I want her to begin with Dianna's need to get away. Second, I'll bring up the idea of him going with them and the reasoning behind the suggestion."

Quint nodded, "Yes, sir. I like it."

Gerald shook his head, "Come off it. We've been friends for too long for you to go sir-ing me."

Quint chortled. "That we have. I'll see you at the White House for that meeting."

"Before you go, did you give Buster a heads-up?"

"I did and he'll go if he must, but he is not happy with the timing."

"Lord, are we interfering with his love life?" Gerald grinned as he knew Buster's proclivities well.

Quint laughed. "Far be it from me to squeal on him."

Gerald laughed as well. "No problem. I get it. I've known Buster a long time, too. One more thing before you go. The janitor lady at the school checked out. When she entered the restroom it was empty. The girls had already climbed out the window."

Quint nodded. "Good. Do you have a lead on who may be helping the perps from inside the agency?"

"Nothing yet. But we're digging."

Quint left Gerald's office to find Murphy in the reception area thumbing through a well-worn magazine. Murphy looked up when Quint walked out. "I'm about starved, so don't even think about leaving until I get a sandwich or something to eat."

Quint flushed with shame that Gerald and he had enjoyed lunch completely forgetting about Agent Murphy. "Tell you what, we'll swing by the café and order you something to go. I'll drive so you can eat. Okay."

"I'm not supposed to allow you to drive, but in this case, I'll let you."

"It's a shame you don't have a chauffeur's cap. You could sit in the backseat and enjoy the ride."

"Screw that. I hate not being the one behind the wheel. I'm the worst backseat driver you ever saw."

Quint groaned, "Spare me. I have enough to deal with just getting through D.C. traffic without a lot of lip from you."

"Then let's fill my mouth with enough to chew on while you're doing the driving. That way I won't be chewing on you."

"Sounds like a plan."

Within twenty minutes, they were on their way back to the White House. Quint swore to himself at the abysmal traffic and was more than relieved to arrive with no more than frayed nerves. He had enough time before the meeting with the President for a quick nap that he badly needed. Murphy and he left the car at the front entrance for the security detail to park. Quint wearily climbed the stairs to his suite with Murphy trooping along behind. He could not help but wonder if the man ever got to sleep except in a chair outside his door. It took a special dedication to the Nation's service for men like Murphy to endure the myriad hardships their jobs entailed. All things considered, he realized his job, while dangerous, held fewer such physical hardships. Chagrined that he could climb into a comfortable bed for a few hours sleep while Murphy could not, Quint turned to Murphy. "Thanks, man. I may not say it often enough, but I appreciate all you are doing to keep me safe."

"No thanks needed. It goes with the turf. But you're welcome."

CHAPTER 20

Lila was standing by her printer smiling when Quint walked into their suite. Holding up a sheet of paper she waved it at him. I have them...the names you wanted and who they are. It's an interesting read for sure."

"Damn! You are an amazing, wonderful woman. How did I get so lucky?" Quint picked her up and whirled her around making her giggle with delight. "Now let's see what you found."

Sitting beside him on the sofa, Lila watched silently as Quint read what she had written:

> 'Medvev...holding company of AtomKaz, Office in Nur-Sultan, Kazakhstan's Capital City.
>
> Alexsei Volkov...Russian born billionaire industrialist residing in Kazakhstan, vacation homes in Miami Beach and Cannes. Chief Operations Officer.
>
> Dimitri Golubev...Russian investment banker residing primarily in Moscow. Chief Financial Officer. Second home is in Nur-Sultan.
>
> Fyodor Mikhailov...Russian born billionaire industrialist residing in Moscow. On the board of both Medvev and the Russian state-owned company of Uranium one. Second home in Tanzania near uranium mine and branch office there. Anatoly Belyaev...Russian

born mining engineer residing in Nur-Sultan.
Jomart Vassilenko...Kazakhstan Ambassador to the
United States. Board member of Medvev.'

Quint whistled when he reached Vassilenko. "That last name on the list is mighty interesting. Did you send this to Gerald?"

"Yes. Immediately once I found the names."

Quint proceeded to tell her about the meeting arrangements Gerald was making before dinner to discuss both Dianna and the President going with Lila to Figure Eight. She chewed at her lips as he talked. Realizing something was bothering her, he stopped.

"What has you worried?"

"Doesn't that make it more dangerous for us at Figure Eight if the President is there? It's not like there will be hundreds of security guards surrounding us like there are here, and we don't have a bunker. Besides, I thought it would be good for Dianna to just get away from all of this." Lila waved her hand around in a circle as she said it.

Quint nodded, "Everything you have said is true. Before we get too worried about the logistics, let's see how the President reacts to Gerald's proposal. He may choose to stay here... especially with what you have discovered." Quint tapped the paper. "I suspect this is going to be a priority at our meeting."

"Dinner is at 7:30. Gerald will probably try to arrange the meeting for 6 or 6:30. He should be texting us shortly with a confirmation of the ETA."

Lila leaned against his shoulder. "It's 3:30 now, and I've done my work for the day. I think we might have time for you to do some of that coddling you promised...as in serious cuddling.

What do you think?"

"What are you waiting for? To the bedroom, woman."
*****

At 6:00, Lila and Quint walked into the Oval Office to find the President and Gerald Williams drinking a stiff shot of Blanton's. Gerald pointed to their waiting glasses on the table and nodded to them to sit. When he greeted them the President's face held both curiosity and foreboding for the necessity of the impromptu meeting.

Once Lila and Quint were seated and had taken a sip of their drinks, President Northrup asked, "What's up, Gerald?"

The CIA director began, "Mr. President, Lila has discovered both the company and the principal partners that we believe are potentially behind the attacks you have experienced since you tried to block uranium imports to Iran and North Korea. We strongly suspect this is the culprit cabal as my own agents have investigated the other companies trading in Aluminum products and find no ties that link back to a Washington or US presence. Whether or not it is the entire Medvev upper hierarchy that is involved remains to be seen."

Northrup turned to Lila, "Great job. Now tell me what you know."

Lila handed the President a copy of the same memo she had provided to Quint and Gerald and waited for him to read it. When he got to the name of the Kazakhstani Ambassador to Washington, he looked up. Disgust was written all over his face when he snarled, "That Fuc..., sorry Lila...that piece of human feces! I never liked or trusted the man."

Turning to Gerald Williams, Northrup asked, "So, how do you suggest we deal with this?"

"Mr. President," Gerald began, "At the moment my bet is that the primary perpetrators leading the assaults are Volkov and Vassilenko in particular. It would be much better to move you to an unknown location until we can stop any further action against you. I strongly recommend that both you and Dianna go with Lila to Figure Eight. Quint's house is on the ocean and is accessed only through a bridge with a gatehouse. We can station our agents on the bridge to the island, in the air, and on both the sea and sound sides. We can also launch drone surveillance, as well as adding additional agents on the ground. Quint has a hidden safe room in case it is needed. I would feel far more comfortable about your safety and that of your daughter if you went on a quiet vacation. Quint's guest house can easily accommodate the agents that will be traveling with you."

Before he could say more, Lila added, "Mr. President, I have spent a lot of time talking to Dianna. She is still traumatized by her kidnapping and the murder of her mother. If we do not find a way for her to relax away from what she sees as a threatening environment, I fear for her mental stability. You are all she has left, and she is worried sick she will lose you, too. This latest attack on the White House only adds to her anxiety. I urge you to consider Director Williams' suggestion. By the way, our housekeeper is a wonderful cook. She will keep you both happy. And nothing is better for morale than Code. He is also very protective."

Northrup wiped his right hand down his face as though he could erase all that had imperiled both him and his family as a consequence of his decision to block the exportation of heavy uranium to enemy countries. If he had to do it over again, he knew he would make the same decision. He had just never imagined the dire consequences of his actions. Hanging his head to hide the tears that had sprung into his eyes, he pondered what he should do. His first reaction was to stay in Washington and confront the Ambassador, but would that be best for his daughter? She had endured more than anyone should have to face because of his position as head of the government.

Looking up, he turned to Gerald, "I think it will be good for Dianna to get away, but would it be better if I stay here and deal with the international ramifications?"

Gerald glanced at Quint before he replied, his voice grim, "I suggest you let Quint and me handle that in our own way. Trust me, we will resolve it and it is best politically and otherwise if you are not involved. You may well need plausible deniability."

Northrup looked first to Quint and then at Lila, "Is this what you recommend...that both Dianna and I go to your home on Figure Eight with Lila?"

They both nodded. Lila smiled before adding, "I have become something of a mother figure to Dianna. She is hurting so much; and worry for your safety only adds to it. Knowing her mother was murdered, she was kidnapped and may have well been murdered, and you have been under attack is unsettling to say the least."

"Say, I agree to this, how do I handle my job from Figure Eight?"

Quint interjected, "Sir, we can set you up with first rate security and connection services. Any decisions, memos, or statements you make can originate from there and no one will know they didn't come from here. Until we stop the perpetrators, I agree with Gerald that this is the best option. I also agree with my wife that Dianna cannot take much more."

"Can you smuggle me out of here so that no one is the wiser? With people everywhere, it is going to take some real magic."

"That's where some play acting, wigs, makeup, glasses, and a different look in clothes comes in handy." Gerald added, "I will see to it you both have everything you need to make you unrecognizable. Quint is an expert at that sort of thing and can help you. The three of you will mingle with a White House tour group and exit with them. We will have an agent, also in disguise meet you at the exit and take you to a plain car...not a recognizable government one. He will drive you. Once we get you away from the White House, he will take you to Langley for the next stage of the trip. I thought a charter bus might be a way to get you, Dianna, and Lila, and the necessary security agents and equipment, to the island. It's a long trek, but doable in a day and I will make sure the bus is comfortable, secure, and well equipped to handle your needs. From the outside, it will look like any other tour bus, but the interior will have the communications equipment and protection your office requires, also restroom, food, etc. With an enlarged gas tank there will be no stopping once you leave Langley until we get you to Figure Eight. The other option is to arrange for a private plane to get you into Wilmington. It takes less time, but it is also more obvious if someone sees you deplane, and then gets suspicious when they see a caravan of cars waiting. Therefore, the bus is my preference."

"I hate to leave with so much that I must do, but I see the sense in it for my daughter's sake. Otherwise, I wouldn't go." Northrup laughed and shook his head. "You might have gotten my okay before you went to such detailed plans."

Gerald could not keep of defensive note from his voice when he replied, "With the culprits still out there, we have no choice but to plan for every contingency." Northrup sighed.

"I'm not scolding. These last few weeks have been hell for all of us. I will tell Dianna at dinner we are going to sneak away for a vacation. Lila, you can fill her in on the details and help Quint with her disguise."

Lila responded, "Thank you. We'll make it fun for her."

"Good. I don't know about the rest of you but I'm ready for some dinner. Gerald, I hope you plan to join us?"

"I would love to Mr. President, but I have a lot to do to pull this off as quickly as possible. I would appreciate a raincheck, sir."

"Any time!"

The President inquired, "Before you go...how soon do Dianna, Lila, and I need to be ready to leave?"

"Tomorrow morning. Tours begin at 7:30. You need to be in the stairway across from the Green Room by 7:50. When the visitors are in the Cross Hall, mingle in. Follow the first ones to leave. I will have the security agent, who will drive you waiting in the stairway for you to come down. He will be with you for the remainder of your time away. The guards on duty tomorrow morning will be our most trusted and will be sworn to total secrecy. I already have the head of security here setting that up. After an early breakfast in your rooms, go to Quint's suite where the wigs, clothes, makeup, etc. you will need will be waiting. He will help you with your disguises and how to alter your body language. Keep the disguise in place until you are inside Quint's house on Figure Eight. When you finish dinner, go to your rooms, and stay there until after your breakfast which will be served in your rooms. Mr. President, I will leave it to you and Lila to fill Dianna in on the details. By the way, pack tonight but take no luggage with you in the morning. We will pick up your luggage late tonight and fly it down. It will be waiting for you when you arrive."

Gerald looked from the President to Lila and Quint. "Any questions?"

Northrup looked thoughtful for a moment before asking, "How do you keep the press from wondering about my whereabouts if I just disappear?"

"We are going to say you have a mild case of COVID and are quarantined in your rooms until you test negative."

"And my daughter?"

"The same." Gerald looked at the three of them, "Anything else?"

When they all shook their heads, Gerald added, "Quint, the minute they are gone, have Murphy drive you to Langley. I will have Buster meet us so we can develop a detailed game plan."

"Will do."

After Gerald left the three of them went to the family dining room where Dianna was waiting outside the door. Northrup said, "I'm sorry we're late, darling. But, we have been planning a vacation so you and I can escape for a few days."

Dianna squealed. The questions came in rapid fire order, "Really? Where are we going? When do we leave? How long are we staying?"

The President laughed. "We are leaving first thing in the morning. We're going to Quint and Lila's house on Figure Eight Island in North Carolina. There is a beach and I hear they have a fabulous housekeeper and cook who will make you all your favorites. You can swim and play on the beach with Code. I'm not sure how long we'll be away, but pack enough for a week or so. You need to do that tonight."

"Wonderful. This is so exciting. I can't wait."

Lila laughed. "One more thing, we are all going to be in disguises and sneak away without anyone knowing."

"We are? What kind of disguise?"

"Quint will have things in our room in the morning and he will help you with disguises. We will be wearing something nondescript and comfortable because it's a long ride."

"Are you and Quint going, too?"

"Just me. Quint has work to do here."

"Cool. I like the idea of some girl time." A look of sadness flickered across her face. Since Barbara had betrayed her and helped with her kidnapping, Dianna had not returned to school or seen any of the other girls she had known there. She had missed having a friend to giggle with and to talk to about the things of interest to girls on the cusp of womanhood. She was beginning to see Lila as a replacement for both her lost girlfriend and mother.

Her father instructed, "We are going to our rooms to pack when we finish dinner. We need to stay put until after breakfast in the morning. Set your clock for six o'clock sharp. I realize that's earlier than you like to get up, but it's important we stick to a tight schedule if we are going to pull this off. We must be in Quint's room no later than 6:30. It's a long ride from here to the island, so you can nap on the bus if you get sleepy."

Dianna's eyes went wide with surprise, "A Bus? Wow. I would never have suspected that."

"And that, my sweet, is the whole idea."

CHAPTER 21

Both the President and his daughter arrived on time for the transformation of their appearances. While Quint worked on Northrup, Lila quickly donned a wig, frumpy sweatpants, hoodie, and sneakers. Dianna giggled when Lila turned around and modeled for her.

Lila warned, "Don't you laugh at me, my girl. Just you wait until you see what I do with you."

In the bathroom President Northrup leaned over the basin while Quint dusted his head with powder. He then painted a light coat of blue under Northrup's eyes and added large horn rim glasses. He then gave the President a pair of large baggy slacks in a faded grey color, a casual lightly wrinkled shirt, and topped it with an outsized navy sweater with liberal pills and picks. The final touch was scuffed brown shoes and a cane. Once he was dressed, Quint showed the President how to roll his shoulders forward and shuffle as he walked. The man looked at least twenty years older. Catching his reflection in the mirror, the President laughed.

"I can't wait until Dianna sees me."

Modeling before the mirror, he snorted. "This is the most fun I have had in years."

Quint chuckled, "Let's see what Lila has done with Dianna." Father and daughter stared at each other before both whooped with laughter. With tears rolling down her face, Dianna studied her transformed father. "You look so old and decrepit. I guess I will have to call you grandpa."

The President bit back a laugh, but his eyes twinkled as he watched Dianna strike a pose for him. Lila had sprayed blue and green dye on Dianna's hair, dressed her in shredded jeans, a cropped camisole, and topped the outfit with a faded jacket. She looked much like many of the teens that toured the White House daily. Wiping his eyes, the President remarked, "This is fun for now, but don't think the President's daughter can do this once our little vacation is over."

Dianna shrugged her shoulders, "Oh, pooh. I think this is just me somehow. It really fits my personality, don't you think?"

Northrup hugged his daughter. "Enjoy it for now. It certainly looks like more fun than your poor old grandpa's get up."

Quint hugged Lila and gave her a kiss. Keeping his voice low for just her ear, he whispered, "I will miss you, but I think this will be great for you three and Code, too. He loves to play on the beach; and I know he has not enjoyed the restrictions here anymore than Dianna has. Give Teresa a hug for me. I hope to resolve this mess and join you soon."

Lila put her hands on both sides of his face, "It's you I worry about. I don't know what Gerald has in mind, and I don't want to know because I would be frantic. I just know it's going to be dangerous. Please, stay safe for me. I love you."

"I love you, too." Giving her a last kiss, Quint turned to the President, "Sir, it's time for y'all to go down the stairs where an agent will be waiting. I hope you will be able to enjoy this little vacation. When you return, we intend for all threats to be neutralized."

The President nodded. "That is my prayer. In the meantime, keep me informed."

Quint hesitated before answering as there was no need for the President to know the particulars of whatever Gerald had in mind. "I'm sure Gerald will keep you updated on all that has pertinence."

"Damn it, Quint. You are beginning to sound like a politician."

"I don't think that was a compliment, sir." Quint chuckled.

The President laughed without replying. Turning to Lila and Dianna, he ordered, "Okay ladies, help the old man down the stairs."

Lila took his elbow, "Be careful 'father.' We wouldn't want you to trip on these steps."

Northrup merely grunted as he used his cane to navigate. Dianna trailed behind. At the foot of the steps, the waiting agent identified himself before motioning them to stay put until he had checked the hallway. Seeing it momentarily clear, he beckoned them to exit the stairwell. In a matter of moments, the four of them were joined by a group of tourists who were leaving the Red Room.

An elderly woman studied them silently before walking up to Northrup. "Excuse me sir, you remind me of someone. For the life of me I can't think who. I'm from Ames, Iowa. Are you from there? I know I have seen your face somewhere."

"I'm sorry, ma'am, but I've never even been to Iowa," Northrup lied. "People have told me I have an ordinary face. Maybe that's it."

"I guess. It surely is a puzzle as I have always had a good memory for faces. I wonder if you are…"

Before she could finish what she was about to say, Dianna

took Northrup by the arm. "Grandad, I want to go back to the Red Room. There is a painting in there I didn't get a chance to see up close because of the people."

Lila agreed, "Let's all take a look."

Turning from the woman who was being nudged toward the Green Room by another older woman, the three of them walked back the way the group had come. The agent trailed them. The minute the tourists were all in the Green Room, he urged them to follow him. Forgetting his cane and stoop, Northrup hurried after the agent with Lila and Dianna on his heels. Soon they were on their way to Langley.

While they were making their escape, Quint locked the door of their suite and joined Murphy who was waiting in the hall. Thinking about what faced them on the ride to Gerald's office, Quint began to jot notes of what they needed to determine to nail the perps. Sammy was still needed for IDing the drone operators. If the boat rental was tied only to one of the two men that Sammy had seen on the boat and not a third party, that was a loose end that needed tying up. If Gerald's agents had discovered that information, he had not yet shared it with Quint. That left the identity of the man Quint killed that infiltrated hospital security and tried to kill Sammy. Was he the one that killed the First Lady? The questions became: could different bad guys all be tied together, and was that a reasonable supposition? That left the persons or person behind the attacks, either Volkov and/or Vassilenko with the AtomKaz company, or others. He then ticked off what he knew: Dianna's kidnapping, with the ones responsible for that dead,

✓ The murder of FLOTUS,

✓ perpetrators or perpetrator unknown,

- ✓ one dead,
- ✓ The attack on Sammy with that perp dead,
- ✓ The attack at the cemetery by the two unidentified drone operators;
- ✓ would Sammy be able to identify them?
- ✓ The attack at the White House,
- ✓ with those three attackers also dead.

Quint stared at his list before ticking off the ones that were dead: Vassily Morosov and Ivan Smirnov. Ivan had died in a car crash following Dianna's kidnapping. Vassily had also been involved in the kidnapping but died as a result of injuries during the White House attack. The other two involved in the White House attack were also dead. Who were they and if...or how... did they all tie into the series of attacks? The photos of the dead would be shown to Sammy Crenshaw to see if he could identify any of them as the two men on the barge. Various methods would be used to determine the identities of the dead using passport control, Interpol, phone records, biometrics where possible, and other governmental resources. That left the hired assassin, Vlad Zavrazhin. Gerald's office was searching to determine his whereabouts. No one matching his description was among the dead.

Gerald was waiting for Quint when he arrived. Buster was already in his office. Gerald motioned Quint to take the other chair in front of his desk. "Gentlemen, before we proceed, do either of you have anything to share?"

Quint handed over his notes saying nothing while Gerald read them over. Gerald laid the list on his desk before commenting, "These are my questions as well. We have identified all three of those involved in the White House attack. They are low level thugs from either Russia or Kazakhstan. We already have photos of them, and my agents will show them to Sammy today. The dead assailant that attacked Sammy was another Russian goon by the name of Yuri Belyaev. He was a known felon who has been on the FBI watch list for years. We have tied him and the other two dead guys from the White House to Vassily Morosov through geo-spatial tracking. My guess is that Morosov was behind most, if not all, of these attacks. The question is to whom did he report? We have another contact on Morosov's phone that we have not yet run to ground. That could well be the one that Morosov reported to. Was this unknown person the one running the operation for Jomart Vassilenko and Alexsei Volkov. We are in the process of procuring a wiretap on Vassilenko's phone and office, and Volkov's phone. Because of Vassilenko's position as Ambassador, it is a little trickier politically to bug his office and get a tap on his phone. However, with what we suspect, we have made as strong a case as we can to the FISA court. That leaves Vlad Zavrazhin. I still have not able to fit him into the puzzle. It's possible he is not involved. The minute we can learn the identities of those behind these attacks, Quint, it is up to you and Buster to neutralize them. I do not want to know the details. It is imperative nothing can lead back to this office or the President."

Quint and Buster glanced at one another; both understood his meaning. They left the Director's office not knowing when they would move to the next stage of the mission. They would be the ones hung out to dry if something went wrong. It went with the turf, but it was never a 'happy ending.' With little to do except wait, they decided to pay a visit to Sammy. Hopefully by the time they arrived, he would have been shown photos of the two unidentified men that died in the attack on the White House. If they were the same ones that Sammy had seen launching the drones and shooting him, that would be one more loose end wrapped up. When they arrived at the cabin in the mountains of Virginia that Gerald often used for a safe house, Sammy was sitting outside under a tree. He was whistling to himself and whittling on a stick. Looking up when they got out of the car, Sammy stood and walked over to them.

"It sure is good to see you two fellers. Y'all been doing good?"

"Were fine, Sammy. How about you?" Quint queried. "Man, what have I got to complain about. I got a couple of guys keeping me company, all the good food I can eat, beer, a roof over my head, television…I could get used to this. Hell, this is like living in a resort I ain't got to pay for. You tell that CIA man he can keep me here as long as he wants to."

Both Quint and Buster laughed, before Buster asked, "Hey man, has anyone shown you photos of two men that might be the ones that shot you?"

"Not yet. Do you think you can nab them?"

Quint replied, "It's possible. It depends on whether you can identify them."

One of the agents staying with Sammy walked out of the house and came over to them. He held up his phone, "The boss just sent me this, Sammy. Take a look at these photos. We need to know if you have seen them before."

Sammy took the agent's phone and studied first one and then the other photo. "Yeah, these are the ones with the drones that shot me."

"Great. I'm going to let Director Williams know you have ID-ed them."

Sammy looked Quint in the eye, "Are they running around

loose so I got to worry about them coming after me?"

Buster shook his head, "Not unless you are worried about being chased by ghosts. These two are dead."

"Iffn I was, I wouldn't a been living in no cemetery."

After the agent returned to the house to call Gerald Williams, Sammy turned to Quint, "Damn. I guess my vacation is over."

Quint shrugged. "I'll see what I can do about you staying here a while, but the two agents are going to be pulled. They will be assigned to other duties now that you are safe."

"I 'spect I might as well go on back to the cemetery. It ain't so bad there. Besides, it would get kinda lonely here without the company."

Both agents emerged from the house with their luggage and began stowing it in their car. Sammy left Quint and Buster and went into the house he had called home for the last few weeks. When he returned to them, he was carrying a pillowcase with what appeared to be groceries.

"Can I go with you and Buster. You know where to drop me off."

"Sure. I'll just let them know you are leaving with us."

After the agents bid Sammy goodbye and told him how much they had enjoyed hearing all his stories, Quint, Buster, and Sammy left the hideaway to drive back to D.C. Once there, they dropped Sammy off at the gate to the cemetery. He waved at them as they drove away. In his pocket was a wad of bills Quint had given him when they stopped. As far as Sammy was concerned, he hadn't minded all that much being shot since it hadn't killed him. The last few weeks had been the most exciting he had had since Nam, and he had new friends that promised to visit from time-to-time to check on him. Shifting the bag of groceries over his shoulder, Sammy began to make his way to the mausoleum he made his home.

Following a late dinner in their suite at the White House, Quint was planted in front of the television watching the news. The regular programing was interrupted by an announcement from Reginald Davis, the White House Spokesman. He explained that the President and his daughter both had a mild case of COVID and were being quarantined until they tested negative for the virus. Davis assured the Nation that the President would continue with his usual duties despite testing positive. At that moment Quint's phone rang. He glanced at the screen and saw it was his wife. "Lila, did you guys make it?"

Lila told him that it was an easy trip, despite the hours it had taken. She explained that the President, Dianna, and the security detail were all in their quarters. Teresa had cooked a lavish fresh seafood dinner and had it waiting when they arrived. Tired and with bellies full, everyone was ready for bed. After Lila had helped clean up and thanked Teresa for the meal, she had gone to the master bedroom to call Quint. They laughed when she told him about the President almost being recognized and how much Northrup and his daughter enjoyed their disguises. In the background, Quint could hear Code bark once. Lila called the dog over and held the phone to his ear so Quint could say hello. After saying goodnight, Quint rolled over and hugged Lila's pillow. He already missed her.

CHAPTER 22

Two days later Gerald Williams looked at (Quint and Buster) who were seated in front of him. He explained that he had already talked with President Northrup to inform him of the information the CIA had learned from the taps on both the Kazakh Ambassador and Alexsei Volkov. Both suspects had communicated with Vlad Zavrazhin, and a wiretap on his phone had provided the link to Vassily Morosov who had facilitated the attacks under Zavrazhin's direction. The bears had been tracked. Now they had to be trapped. The President and CIA Director Williams devised a plan to diplomatically resolve the prominent participants in the plot to destroy Northrup and end his ban on exports to US enemies that could be used to develop nuclear weapons.

A discrete call by President Northrup to the President of Kazakhstan resolved the issue with the Ambassador. Jomart Vassilenko would return home for what was supposedly an official visit. There he would quietly and permanently disappear. The same fate would be assured for Alexsei Volkov who would be summoned by the Kazakh President for a discussion on how to further develop the mining industry in Kazakhstan.

"There is a new member of the cabal we discovered with the wiretaps. Dimitri Golubev, board member and sometime resident of Kazakhstan, is a Russian national. He is in this scheme as deep as the other two. President Northrup called the Russian President and explained what was happening. He assures us that he will deal with Golubev, who is currently in Moscow. Both Russian and Kazakhstan officials are relieved to have suspicion removed from their countries and instead placed on the three AtomKaz officers. I suspect someone will arrange for AtomKaz to be bought out by one of the other companies mining ore in Kazakhstan. Diplomatically, we could not ask for a better outcome. That leaves just one more loose end…the assassin and mastermind that implemented the attacks. I have Vlad Zavrazhin's address. Your job is to arrange for his permanent disappearance."

Buster snorted. "He's as slippery as goose shit. Zavrazhin has managed to elude or kill everyone that has ever gone after him. Interpol has been after him for years and can't nail his ass."

"If it were easy, I would not have turned it over to you and Quint to resolve."

Buster rolled his eyes, "Yeah, yeah."

Gerald shook his head. "Such enthusiasm, Buster. At least, you are not going to be sent to Kazakhstan."

"That's real nice. But, I have to tell you I would rather tangle with a mad bear than this Russian assassin."

"Buster, you and Quint are the best I have. I trust you to take care of this for me." Gerald turned to Quint. "You aren't saying much."

"What's to say. You have given us a job. We have to figure out how to do it. I want every photo and every scrap of information you have on this guy. We are going to need every bit of help we can get. He is one dangerous dude."

"You'll have it. We are working on his file now to update details. I'll see to it that any street cameras within blocks of the gym go down for a thirty-minute window. If you need more than that, it will mean the whole thing went sour. Murphy is no longer assigned to you, so it will just be you and Buster. Now, the two of you go have a drink." Gerald added, "Sounds like Buster needs some Dutch courage."

Buster growled, "Dammit. That kind of comment is enough to make me resign. If I didn't owe you for past favors, I would. This crap gets old. If this Zavrazhin doesn't kill me, I just may quit."

"Have faith, Buster. You know I trust your ability to handle whatever I throw at you."

Quint interjected, "We may both quit. I'm ready to sit on my ass on the beach, make love to my wife, walk my dog, and just enjoy life. I'm tired of putting my life and Lila's at risk."

"Take care of business first. I'll let you know when we have the file ready." Gerald laughed before adding, "You guys know you would miss all the excitement I provide."

As they stood to leave, Buster rolled his eyes. His voice laden with sarcasm, Buster replied, "Fun I could use. This kind of 'excitement' I can do without."

The phone rang long before Quint's alarm sounded the next morning. Rolling over, he picked his phone up from the bedside table and glanced at the screen before answering. It was Gerald letting him know that he was texting both him and Buster the information they had on Vlad Zavrazhin. The Director again emphasized the need for discretion even though he knew it was unnecessary as Quint and Buster had cleaned up problems in the past that the Director needed to disappear quietly. He then outlined the hit that he had planned. In thirty minutes, an agent met Quint at the exit of the White House with a package containing clothes and poison. Cautioning Quint to handle it with care, he explained how to use the poison. "If you two get caught, you know you are on your own."

"We know the drill."

In an hour, Buster and Quint were on the way to the gym where Vlad went every morning to work out. According to the file they were given the man was punctual in his exercise routine, arriving at 6:00 and leaving at 7:00. They were to apprehend him when he left the gym to walk back to his apartment. With them they carried two syringes that were in the package. Both were filled with deadly Batrachotixin neurotoxin derived from the Latin American poison dart frog. Only one was necessary. Two was a safeguard. Quint carried one. Buster had the other. Vlad was strong with finely honed instincts. He would not have survived long if he had not had them. They realized they would get only one chance to inject him. It had to be done quickly before the man became alarmed and could defend himself.

They parked their car a block from the gym on the route to Vlad's apartment house. The street was deserted at that hour and heavy fog helped to hide any activity. At two minutes before 7:00, they left the car and began walking toward the gym. Both Quint and Buster were dressed in worker uniforms identifying them as utility repair men. Quint carried a toolbox in his left hand and the syringe in his right. Buster carried his syringe in his left hand.

Right on time, Vlad Zavrazhin left the gym and began walking towards them. Quint turned like he was studying building numbers, separating himself from Buster so Vlad would walk between them. When he drew even with them, Quint swung the toolbox catching Vlad in the leg. "Son of a Bitch! Watch out, you fool," Vlad snarled.

Quint stuttered and apology, "I-I'm real sorry. I-I hope I

didn't hurt you?"

Vlad snarled, "No. Now get out of my way."

Vlad was so focused on Quint he did not see Buster raise his arm and plunge the needle deep into his neck. The man flinched and began to lift his hand to swat at whatever had bitten him. In mid-movement, his knees gave way, and he sank to the pavement. Quint then injected Vlad with the second syringe. Quint and Buster hurried to hoist him up and drag him to the car. Glancing around Quint searched to see if anyone had seen what was happening. Relieved that it had gone so smoothly, they tossed the inert body into the rear seat and drove away. The infamous assassin would kill no more.

Driving deep into the swampy woods of Maryland, they turned down a gravel road that led to a creek. Pulling the body from the car, they watched in silence as the dead man sank into the tannin dark waters, both lost in their own thoughts.

Quint turned to Buster, "He deserved what he got, but it I still hate this part of the job."

Buster's voice was somber, "Tell me about it! I don't know about you, but after this little excursion I could use a stiff drink with lunch."

"I'm in. I'll call Gerald and let him know his problem is taken care of." Quint added, "After that drink, I'm catching the first plane to Wilmington and my house on Figure Eight. It's time I went home. If you want a vacation, come on down."

"Well, thanks for the offer, but I'm going to stick around here. I've been out a couple of times with that lady I mentioned. So far, she looks really promising."

Quint chuckled, "Long term, or short term?"

Buster laughed, "With me, who knows!"

Title: *Run Cissy Run*

- Betty J. vaughn
- Language: English
- Hard Cover Book ISBN: 9781590956748
- Paper Back Book ISBN: 9781590956755
- eBook / ePub: ISBN: 9781590956762

Book One

You would think Cecilia LaRoque has it all: a loving father, wealth, beauty, social position and a devoted suitor. She doesn't. Crushed by a cold and critical mother who soon absconds to live with a dissolute lover, 'Cissy' struggles to prove herself worthy of love and respect. She could not have foreseen in her teenage years that the genteel and privileged life she had led would come to a crashing halt with the outbreak of Civil War, a bitter struggle that would tear her world apart. Despite the hardships and inherent danger, she seizes the opportunity to forge an unorthodox role for herself as a spy.

Reviews for *Run Cissy Run*

"*Run, Cissy, Run* is a great book. Trust me, you will not want to put it down."

--*Ann Compton*

"Just finished reading *Run, Cissy, Run*! Enjoyed it very much!"
--*Edie H. Bailey*

"I just finished reading *Run, Cissy, Run* and enjoyed it a lot. I like that there is southern history as well as the story, as a lot of it I do not know."

--*Sharon E. Brumbaugh*

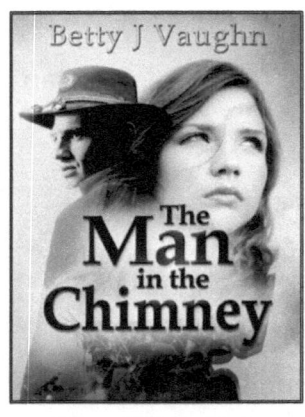

Title: *The Man In The Chimney*

- Betty J. vaughn
- Language: English
- Hard Cover Book ISBN: 9781590956021
- Paper Back Book ISBN: 9781590956038
- eBook / ePub: ISBN: 9781590956045

Book Two

The War Between the States has come to eastern North Carolina, bringing hardships, pillaging, and fear to the local residents. For those left at home, the struggle to procure the needs of daily life is all-consuming; for those serving in the armies of both North and South, death is a daily companion. Against this backdrop, an unlikely and forbidden love affair between a local woman and a Union officer leads to difficult choices for them both—choices that will tear them apart and force them to deal with the abandonment of their dream of a life together.

Despite broken hearts, misunderstandings, and missed chances, Penny and Ryan strive to survive the dangers and ravages of war and make the best of their separate futures. With the surrender of the South at Appomattox, Penny realizes she has one last chance to either find the man she loves or settle for a life alone.

Reviews for *The Man In The Chimney*

"I read *The Man in the Chimney* and loved it. What a beautiful romance Penny and Ryan enjoyed! I look forward to reading the next in the series."

--*Elaine Werner*

"I read *The Man in the Chimney* and *Turbulent Waters*. My favorite part was the author's descriptions of the things the people lived through and how they coped."

--*Leesa Payne*

"The *Man in the Chimney* was fabulous. I could not put it down."

--*Cyndi McNeill*

Title: *Turbulent Waters*
- Betty J. vaughn
- Language: English
- Hard Cover Book ISBN: 9781590951743
- Paper Back Book ISBN: 9781590951750
- eBook / ePub: ISBN: 9781590951767

Book Three

LOVE IS PERSONAL, WAR IS NOT, especially in North Carolina, 1865-1867, during the reconstruction. With a love they are certain will transcend all else, southern belle Penny Kennedy marries Union Officer and attorney, Ryan Madison, despite the condemnation of those around them. The initial days of wedded bliss end abruptly when Marcus, the man who courted Penny for years in anticipation that she would marry him, is arrested for murder, and Ryan is assigned to prosecute him. As hard as this development is to tolerate for Penny, she will discover worse things await her before Ryan and she can attain the life they desire.

Reviews for *Turbulent Waters*

"A sigh of relief was enjoyed when the last page of this book had been read as it fulfilled the desire for a prequel to the author's last two award-winning books, covering an area not discussed in the other books and containing data that preceded incidents in the other books, dealing with the Civil War and the Naval campaign. Many times stories of this war don't even touch on the navy's contributions, nor life in the seaport towns that saw more action than we are led to believe.

--Judge: North Carolina Society of Historians - Elizabeth Sherrill

Historical Novel Writing At Its Best!

What a fabulous read! Ms. Vaughn has really done her research for this, and the other two books, in this series! Set in central and northern North Carolina at the beginning of the Civil War, events continue to unfold for Ryan, the Northern office, and Penny, the Southern lady. Just when you believe things have settled down a bit, more conflict arises in their lives!

Turbulent Waters is actually the 3nd book in the 4-book series. The first book, *Run Sissy Run*: than *Man in The Chimney*, introduces us to Penny and her family, and Ryan. Again, it tremendously researched novel of the times and conflicts found in everyday life. When you think you know what will happen, you don't.

"The author's intense research is evident in all of her historical books. But her ability to keep you on the edge of your seat until the very last page is what makes her books truly shine."

--Paulette B. Wright

Title: *The Intrepid Miss LaRoque*
- Betty J. vaughn
- Language: English
- Hard Cover Book ISBN: 9781590957103
- Paper Back Book ISBN: 9781590957110
- eBook / ePub:: ISBN: 9781590957127

Book Four

When Wilmington falls in February of 1865, Cissy LaRoque no longer needs to spy. That will not stop her from finding a new career where she can prove her worth beyond societal expectations of a woman. With the war drawing to an end and Wilmington occupied, she is faced with desperate circumstances. Ryan Madison, a Union officer from the past, and Brandon McLean, a new one, attempt to help her. While attracted to them both, she is aware of family and community hostility toward the enemy and dares not act on the attraction. Her fiancé, Logan who is fighting for the southern cause, does not arouse her ardor like the two Union men. When the Confederacy falls, she convinces her father to allow her to run his shipping office in New Berne while he maintains the main office in Wilmington. There she discovers Ryan has married and Logan has jilted her. Provoked and titillated by a man she cannot have but craves, she puts aside romance and concentrates on business. Despite her father's initial objections, much to his surprise she succeeds far beyond any expectation. Although she is happy in what she has achieved, she is frustrated by what she has lost.

Reviews for *The Intrepid Miss LaRoque*
Excellent book
--James W. Chesnutt

One of the very best Civil War women spy novels ever written. As a Civil War buff you cannot pass this novel up.
Great read, just could not put it down.
Looking forward to the next Cissy LaRoque adventure.
--Hero Judson

Title: *Yesterday's Magnolia*
- Betty J. vaughn
- Language: English
- Hard Cover Book ISBN: 9781590955543
- Paper Back Book ISBN: 9781590955550
- eBook / ePub: ISBN: 9781590955567

Jo envies Margo and Maurice for their ready charm, looks, wealth, glamour, and exciting lives never realizing that it is she who is envied for a life that contains the things that they themselves long for and have not attained.

"It's a shame to have so damned much and yet so little." An eastern North Carolina farmer's daughter, Margot, streaks like a comet into the life style of the rich and famous. Her beauty and exuberant, zestful personality gain her entrance to boardrooms, the White House, a corporate jet stocked with Cristal champagne and caviar, a villa in Italy, and marriage to one of the world's most powerful men. Maurice, the spurned suitor, seeks friendship and comfort from Margot's sister, Jo, a quiet, bookish art history teacher. Jo envies them both for their ready charm, looks, wealth, glamour, and exciting lives never realizing that it is she who is envied for a life that contains the things that they themselves have not attained. Like the comets they so resemble both Margot and Maurice are consumed by the friction of life, leaving Jo to remember the magic moments they brought to a more conventional path.

Reviews for *Yesterday's Magnolia*

This was the perfect read during my beach vacation!! It is very much a vicarious escape to Europe similar to "A Year in Province" and "Under the Tuscan Sun" but with a bit more sex thrown in.
--*Susan White*

"The author engages her readers to the last page."
--*Carolyn Asaki*

Title: *Tiger's Code*

- Betty J. vaughn
- Language: English
- Hard Cover Book ISBN: 9781590953907
- Paper Back Book ISBN: 9781590953914
- eBook / ePub: ISBN: 9781590953921

Quint Cord Series Book One

Quint Cord's latest CIA assignment is proving to be his most challenging and could well lead to catastrophic events if he does not break the code in time to avert them.

Quint Cord is an unlikely spy. With sufficient family money so that he never needs to work, he could have spent his life idling on a beach chasing women. But from the moment he discovers famous codes of the past in a university class, he is hooked. His unique talent for creating and breaking codes brings him to the attention of the CIA.

A powerful and ambitious politician, who's in cahoots with a Saudi prince, plans to seize the US presidency and throw the western world into turmoil. Quint flees the country only to stay one step ahead of a foe determined to kill him before he can break the code.

Clue by clue, Quint begins to zero in on his target but can he stop him in time?

Reviews for *Tiger's Code*

"What a terrific read! The characters are full, and the pace is gripping. I have been a huge fan of Vince Flynn and Tiger's Code is right up there with believable political greed and national security threats that are entirely contemporary. I can't wait to read the next volume in the Quint Cord series."

--*D. L. Soderburg*

"Just finished Tiger's Code: the author moves from historical novels to action packed drama with great skill!!!! Really enjoyed the fast-moving pace."

--*April S. Blizzard*

"Tiger's Code was a fabulous book. I look forward to reading your newest book in the series."

--*Sherry P. Riley*

"Tiger's Code is the first book of fiction I've read in decades. The book is exceptionally well done and kept me interested throughout. I am very impressed with the significant amount of research done to make the information in the book realistic. A great movie could be made from this book's story line. I am buying the next one."

--*Thomas Smith*

Title: *Dragon's Sword*

- Betty J. vaughn
- Language: English
- Hard Cover Book ISBN: 9781590953808
- Paper Back Book ISBN: 9781590953815
- eBook / ePub: ISBN: 9781590953822

Quint Cord Series Book Two

Quint Cord returns to the CIA when his fiancée is almost killed by an egomaniacal hacker who is determined to use his GPS satellite implanted virus to gain control of governments and transportation networks around the globe. Aided by a North Korean dissident who vows to bring down the Kim Jong Un regime, the hacker uses the North Korean's information to crash ships and missiles in Korea and Japan. The hacker next turns to his own country of China to create friction with the United States. When the North Korean becomes frightened for his life and defects, the hacker flees China for fear he will be exposed. Lila Carson, Quint's fiancée, is again on the trail of the hacker as he goes dark to elude discovery.

From North Carolina to Japan and China, and then to Seattle, Quint struggles to capture the man before he can commit more murder and chaos.

Reviews for *Dragon's Sword*

"The book is a quick read because it is so interesting. The author has a real talent for capturing the reader's attention and sustaining that momentum throughout the course of the book."
--Dr. Judith Conway Gordon, Retired English Professor

"I loved Dragon's Sword!! Great action and pace. I didn't want it to end, but alas, it did and now I look forward to the next Quint Cord book."
--D. L. Soderburg

"Dragon's Sword is a good read. Informative and yet fast paced."
--Clay Brumbaugh

"Loved Dragon's Sword and couldn't put it down."
--Lou Cunningham

"Dragon's Sword was so good. Totally going to get the next one in the series."
--Kathy M. Jobe

"Another GREAT book! I just finished Dragon's Sword---couldn't put it down. I enjoyed the suspense and intrigue and can only imagine it may seem only too real to our intelligence community. Well done! I look forward to the next book in the Quint Cord series."
--Elizabeth Atwater

Title: *Lyon's Claw*

- Betty J. vaughn
- Language: English
- Hard Cover Book ISBN: 9791590958000
- Paper Back Book ISBN: 9781590955598
- eBook / ePub: ISBN: 9781590955604

Quint Cord Series Book Three

Lila and Quint Cord are honeymooning in the south of France when Lila is kidnapped. Seized because of her hacking expertise, her captor plans to use her in a deadly game of revenge. While Quint and three CIA operatives work to free her, another and more dangerous plot unfolds with global implications. With hired assassins on their heels, Quint and the other agents must discover what secrets led to the enmity between Lila's captor and his nemesis, recover Lila, and stop the realization of a deadly plot.

Reviews for *Lyon's Claw*

"Great Books! You write one suspenseful thriller right after another. It is difficult for an author to capture my attention to the extent that I do not want to stop reading, but you have succeeded in doing that. The Quint Cord book series would make wonderful movies that would keep the audience on the edge of their seats."

--Dr. Judith Gordon

"This gifted author of eight books is adept at writing nail-biting thrillers that sustain excitement and reader interest from cover to cover."

--Joanna Meredith

"Another GREAT book! I just finished Dragon's Sword---couldn't put it down. I enjoyed the suspense and intrigue and can only imagine it may seem only too real to our intelligence community. Well done! I look forward to the next book in the Quint Cord series Lyon's Claw."

--Elizabeth Atwater

Title: *Bear Tracks*
- Betty J. vaughn
- Language: English
- Hard Cover Book ISBN: 9781648831911
- Paper Back Book ISBN: 9781648832581
- eBook / ePub: ISBN: 9781648832598

Quint Cord Series Book Four

Despite looking forward to a respite from his work with the CIA, Quint Cord is ordered back to Washington by the Director, Gerald Williams, when the President and his family come under attack by unknown forces following his embargo on heavy uranium destined for the country's enemies. When the President's daughter is kidnapped, the Cords move into the White House to assist in locating her. Quint, intuitive and trained in counterterrorism, and Lila a leading expert in computer hacking, have both earned the President's trust through their commitment and expertise in solving other cases. Despite increased security, threats against the President and his family escalate. It takes a few lucky breaks and a lot of investigation to learn who is behind the carnage. The issue becomes how to stop the perpetrators of the attacks without creating an international incident.

Reviews for *Bear Tracks*

Bear Tracks, the latest fiction thriller by Betty Vaughn, focuses on the most recent harrowing case assigned to newly married Quint and Lila Cord. Because of Quint's experience and success as a CIA agent, and his wife's expertise as a computer hacker, they are a logical choice for difficult assignments by CIA director, Gerald Williams.

What could be more critical and menacing on the world stage than a threat to national security and the President's own family? This novel is an action-packed thriller, an exciting escapade, and a nail-biter from beginning to end as Quint and Lila work to stop the perpetrators who are imperiling the First Family and upsetting international dynamics.

--Dr. Judith C. Gordon, Ed.D.

Mrs. Vaughn's latest Quint Cord novel is a masterful weaving together of an exciting and plausible plotline with current international dynamics. You will want to start this book early in the morning as you will not sleep until you have completed this one.

--Bruce Moran, Author / Publisher

Cord is challenged to use every tool at his command to stop the perpetrators behind unrelenting attacks on the President and his family. This fast-paced novel captures the reader's interest from the beginning and holds it to the end.

--Hero Judson

"A Great believable Story! Betty writes one suspenseful thriller right after another. Looking forward to her next one.

--Jessica Tate, Author of *The Macaw Series*